A Turkey
Day
Gathering

A Turkey Day Gathering

From the Editors
Of *True Story* And
True Confessions

Published by True Renditions, LLC

True Renditions, LLC
105 E. 34th Street, Suite 141
New York, NY 10016

Copyright @ 2013 by True Renditions, LLC

ISBN: 978-1-938877-84-1

Visit us on the web at www.truerenditionsllc.com.

Contents

A Holiday Story For "Blended" Families:
SWEET POTATOES AND STEPDAUGHTERS
Our Turkey Day started out badly, till we
learned how to love and listen. . . .

"Thanksgiving is dumb," Brianna said with the same scowl
she seemed to wear all the time.

I was trying to love Paul's daughter. I was having a hard time
even liking her. Right from the start, she'd made it obvious that she
didn't like me.

I plopped down the dough for piecrust and started rolling it
out. I'd thought it would be fun for Brianna to help me get ready for
Thanksgiving, but she was very cynical for ten years old.

"Why is Thanksgiving dumb?" I asked. Why am I going to all
the trouble of making all of this food for you, then? is what I wanted
to ask, but I was trying to be patient.

"Not everybody has things to be thankful for, you know," she
said sullenly. "There're a lot of people who don't even have enough
to eat."

"So we can be thankful that we do," I said firmly, but it was clear
that Brianna didn't feel thankful to be with us. Considering how much
time, money, trouble, and heartache Paul had spent to bring this about,
it was a shame.

"Why would you feel thankful?" Brianna asked, snorting. "Your
baby died."

My heart squeezed painfully. I didn't know what to say. I didn't
think that Brianna was intentionally trying to be cruel, because she often
did try to be cruel and I knew when she was doing it. Now, I realized,
she was just uttering what she saw as the truth, plain and simple.

"Maybe we both feel sad," I said, giving in to her gloom. "But
this Thanksgiving means a lot to your daddy and we're going to
celebrate it."

Brianna made a derisive noise. "I'm going to go on the
computer," she said.

That was another thing we didn't have in common. Brianna is a
ten-year-old computer whiz; I can barely read my email. And Brianna
never failed to show her contempt for my lack of computer literacy.
She'd been living with us for six days and it felt like six months.

I went on making pies by myself, having the kinds of daydreams

1

I'd been having since before Grace, my baby, died during childbirth last year. The irony was that the fantasies I had about Grace, even when I was pregnant, were not of a baby, but of a little girl about Brianna's age. A little girl whose hair I could braid. A little girl whom I could have tea parties with and give dolls to. A little girl to whom I could pass on my beloved, old children's books. But Brianna was nothing like Grace would've been—or how I thought Grace would've been. In my daydreams, Grace said things like, "Thanksgiving is so much fun, Mommy! Can we make two kinds of pie?"

Paul got home from work just as I finished the pies. His ex-wife had given us little notice and subsequently, he hadn't been able to get vacation time. Luckily, my boss was willing to give me my two-week vacation right when I asked for it, at the very last minute.

"Smells wonderful in here," Paul said, kissing the back of my neck.

I turned around and put my arms around him while holding my flour-covered hands away. "Don't get too excited," I said. "The pies are for tomorrow, and so are all of those covered dishes in the fridge. We're going out for pizza tonight."

"The least I can do to thank you for all of this work you're doing is take you out for pizza." He kissed the tip of my nose. "Where's Brianna?"

When asked, Brianna said she didn't like pizza and she wasn't hungry. Paul, as always, ignored her surliness and smiled and jollied her along. Sometimes it seemed like he didn't even notice how unpleasant she was.

Brianna's mother and Paul had divorced seven years ago. Debby was bitter and ever since the divorce, she'd been trying to keep Brianna and Paul apart. Paul had spent a lot of money on lawyers to get joint custody. Then, just as he was about to get it, Debby had moved two thousand miles away without warning. Paul went back to court—in two states. He flew to visit Brianna every couple of months but Debby kept trying to keep them apart. Paul would often fly all the way out there, only to find that Debby had taken Brianna away for the weekend. Needless to say, the bitterness had been hard on Brianna.

Then suddenly, Debby decided to get married again and Brianna was in the way. Debby was currently on her honeymoon. Brianna had been given two weeks off from school to come see her father, since she was a good student. She was doing some schoolwork while she was with us. The visit wasn't going well, but Paul seemed to be ignoring that fact. He was talking about the possibility of getting sole custody of Brianna—or at least having her with us summers.

2

Even now, as Brianna sat in the backseat looking bored, Paul was giving her a tour of town. He did this every time they went out. He called it "learning about your hometown."

"That's the hospital where you were born," he said, pointing down a side street as we were stopped for a light. "I'll never forget that night."

That's the hospital where Grace died, I thought to myself.

"Big deal," Brianna said. "Everybody gets born somewhere."

Two blocks later, Paul pointed to an apartment house, one of the few big ones around. "That's where we lived when you were little," he said.

Brianna actually leaned forward to look. "You mean, you and Mom?"

"And you," Paul said. "You were really little. You probably don't remember."

Brianna sat back. "Mom says it was a dump."

That left even cheerful Paul wordless. We went to the diner instead of the pizzeria since Brianna didn't like pizza. Two hours later, back at home, Brianna was back on the computer while Paul and I watched a kid's movie that we'd rented for her.

"I don't think you should ignore her rudeness like you do," I said to Paul later, as we got ready for bed.

"She'll come around if we're patient with her."

"You've been saying that for almost a week."

He sighed. "What do you want me to do, Kimber? Give up on my own daughter?"

"I'm just saying that we don't seem to be getting anywhere with her."

"She's just a little girl, Kimber." Paul sounded angry, which is unusual for him. "She's had a very rough time of it. First, her father seemed to abandon her—even though I didn't, I know it must've seemed that way to her. And now her mother—"

"I understand all that, Paul. Don't you think I want to love her?"

"I think you're forgetting who the grownups are around here. Your feelings are hurt because she isn't responding to you, but she's the hurt child, and we're the grownups who're supposed to be helping her."

That stung. It was true that I was letting Brianna hurt my feelings instead of thinking about how to help her. Oh, if only she weren't so angry and obnoxious!

Paul came across the room and put his arms around me. "I'm sorry, honey. I know you're still going through a rough time yourself. I'm just so worried about Brianna." He sighed. "All these years of trying to get just a chance to be her father, and now it isn't going well."

3

"I think it would be going better if I weren't here."

"Maybe, but you're part of my life, too, and Brianna has to learn to deal with that."

"I'll try harder," I said.

I woke up early Thanksgiving morning, much as I had so often since Grace died. It was still dark out; I stayed in the warm bed for a while, listening to Paul's quiet snoring and daydreaming about Grace. I imagined that we were stuffing the turkey together and talking about my favorite childhood storybooks.

I'd given Brianna my beloved old copy of The Secret Garden by Frances Hodgson Burnett. I thought she might like it since it was about a sullen little girl nobody wants who finds a secret garden that makes her happy. I hadn't seen her reading it, though, and she certainly hadn't mentioned it.

At breakfast, Paul said, "I want to go and visit Dorothy today. Do you mind if I stick you with all the preparations for dinner?"

"No, but try to be back by two. I want to have dinner at three." Dorothy was Paul's foster mother who'd raised him after his parents were killed in a car crash. She was in a nursing home with Alzheimer's and didn't often even recognize him, but Paul visited her frequently and always on holidays. It was a long drive out and back.

"Can I come?" Brianna asked. Count on Brianna to want to do the one thing Paul wouldn't want her to do.

"Princess, this is something I'd better do by myself," Paul told her gently.

Brianna dropped her fork on top of her uneaten pancakes. "Never mind. I'd rather go on the computer, anyway." She got up to leave the room.

"Brianna, I'd like you to ask to be excused when we aren't done eating," Paul said. "And I'd like you to help Kimber get our big feast ready today."

"Can I be excused?" she asked in a sarcastic voice, and then stalked out of the room.

After Paul left, I sat at the kitchen table drinking coffee and looking out the sliding doors. We had the ground-floor "garden" apartment, though we hadn't done much with the garden yet. It looked very dead this time of year, but I was imagining myself out there with Grace.

"Shall we have tulips or daffodils?" I asked Grace.

Her face was aglow with enthusiasm. I'd bought her little gardening tools of her own. "Oh, let's have both!" she cried excitedly.

I had the turkey stuffed and in the oven a little after ten when Brianna came back into the kitchen. "I'm hungry," she announced sourly.

4

"That's because you didn't eat your breakfast." Then I remembered my promise to Paul to try harder. "I'll make you some oatmeal."

"Icky."

"I'll put in some raisins and brown sugar. It'll taste like oatmeal cookies."

Brianna sat down at the table and waited to be served. We were both silent while I made the oatmeal. I just couldn't think of anything to talk to her about anymore.

"I don't know why you're cooking all this food," she said as I put the bowl of oatmeal in front of her. "There's only me and you and Daddy."

I laughed. "You're right. I guess I'm cooking a dinner the size my mother used to make. Anyway, it wouldn't seem like Thanksgiving without all the food."

"Where's your mother?"

"My parents live in Florida now. My sister lives too far away to come; she and my mother came when . . . they came last year." They came when Grace died. I didn't want to say it.

Brianna ate her oatmeal. "They came to see you when your baby died, didn't they?"

I felt a flash of anger. Why did she keep bringing up Grace's death? Paul felt we should give Brianna an honest answer when she asked us why we didn't have any kids, but I wished now that we'd never told her.

"Yes," I answered. "Don't you want to get outside a little? It's not too cold today, and you can't spend all of your time in front of that computer."

"Daddy says I can't go out on the street by myself."

"I can't leave the turkey," I said, "but you could go in our garden." I gestured to the sliding doors that led outside.

Brianna sneered. "It doesn't look like any garden to me."

"It's November," was my lame answer. "You can pretend it's summer."

"There's no sense in pretending that things are different than they are," she said, like a cynical old lady instead of a little girl.

I didn't have any answer for that.

"It won't help me to pretend that Mommy isn't married to Don now. It won't help you to pretend that your baby is still alive."

"Stop that, Brianna! My baby is none of your business!"

Brianna looked frightened for a minute and I would've apologized for shouting at her, but then her face turned angry and she flounced from the room. Back to her computer, no doubt.

I poured myself a cup of coffee and tried to calm down. Out of the mouths of babes, I thought.

5

I knew it helped me to daydream about Grace—helped me to heal in some small, strange way. But I had to admit that it probably wasn't helping me to keep on doing it. After all, eventually, Paul and I would have another baby. Even if it were a girl, she probably wouldn't turn out much like my "daydream daughter," because life just never is very much like your daydreams.

I went on preparing our dinner. I set the table with our best china and an embroidered, white, linen tablecloth and candlesticks. It didn't look much like a Thanksgiving table with only three places set, but we would do our best. I thought about going in and trying to talk to Brianna, to tell her that I'd yelled at her because she'd hurt me. The surprising thought came to me that she would probably understand that; Brianna was so rude because she hurt so much.

Maybe later, I thought with a sigh, reluctant to tangle with her yet again. Oddly enough, yelling at Brianna had actually made me feel like I understood her better.

Paul got home around two. "Where's Brianna?" he asked after he kissed me. He asked that same question every day when he got home, as though Brianna should be running to the door to fling herself in his arms the minute he walked in.

"At the computer, no doubt."

"You left the front door unlocked when you took the garbage out again," Paul said. "I wish you wouldn't do that."

"Ha. I didn't take the garbage out. You must've left it open."

"No. I locked it." He looked at me, puzzled. "Brianna. . . ."

"She knows she's not supposed to go out alone, Paul."

"Brianna?" Paul called.

No answer.

We searched the house. No Brianna. Her coat was missing.

"She must be outside, around the building somewhere," Paul said. "I'll go look for her."

While he was gone, I looked in all of the closets and under the beds. I could remember hiding when I was angry back when I was a kid, but Brianna was nowhere to be found and Paul still wasn't back. I finally went out and searched the apartment building from top to bottom. It was only three floors and Brianna wasn't on any of them. I ran into two neighbors who helped me look. Paul came back just as I got back to our apartment.

"She's not at Coleston's, either," he said. Coleston's was the convenience store on the corner. "Why would she leave?" He ran his fingers through his hair. He looked frantic.

"I yelled at her," I said, as we went back into the living room.

Paul's face darkened. "Why the heck would you yell at her? I'm going to call the police."

6

The police told Paul to go right down to the station and file a missing persons report. I started to put my coat on to accompany him.

"You stay here," Paul said, "in case she calls."

"She doesn't know our number."

"She has the same last name as we do, and we're listed. Maybe somebody will find her. What time did you see her last?"

"Around ten-thirty."

"You didn't see her for over three hours and you didn't think to check up on her?"

"She's in front of that computer for hours. . . ." I began lamely, but Paul wasn't listening. He was already out the door.

I went into the kitchen and sat at the table. Anguished, I lowered my face into my hands and started to pray. After awhile, the sound of sizzling reminded me of the turkey. I took it out of the oven and put it on the counter to cool. It was done, but there was nobody around to eat it.

The doorbell rang.

"Mrs. Marsden?" the uniformed policewoman asked. "I'm Officer Woolsey. I'm here to help you with some things related to your daughter's disappearance."

Officer Woolsey settled down in the living room by the phone. She told me to call her Pat, and then she went over the description Paul had given of what Brianna was wearing. She called in a couple of corrections I made to that to her dispatcher.

"Now, what I need is to get as much background information as possible so that maybe we can figure out where she might've gone."

I shrugged helplessly. "There isn't anyplace for her to go. This isn't like the big city. Everything's closed on Thanksgiving except for a couple of convenience stores. I can't believe she's not just somewhere close around here."

"We have several teams out looking for her right now, Mrs. Marsden. Your husband is helping them. We're also checking the whole building, but I'm thinking maybe she went to a friend's house or a relative's?"

I shook my head. "We don't have any relatives around here, and Brianna doesn't have any friends."

Officer Woolsey looked surprised.

"Brianna is just visiting her father," I hastened to explain. "She's my stepdaughter, actually. She hasn't lived here long, so she doesn't really know anybody around here."

"Sometimes that's a situation that might be troubled." She was obviously trying to probe tactfully.

"I yelled at her," I admitted, blushing furiously with shame. I wanted to tell her that Brianna was rude and ungrateful and anybody

7

in their right mind would yell at her, but in that moment of chagrin, I knew that Paul was right; I was the grownup and Brianna was the hurt and angry child. It was up to me to help her deal with her feelings, not to make things worse for her.

"I have two kids and I yell at them sometimes," Officer Pat said. "Don't let it get you down. I'm just trying to be sure that Brianna went off by herself because she was upset or angry."

I nodded, slightly relieved. "I'm sure she went by herself. What worries me is if somebody . . . if she met up with somebody. . . ." I couldn't bring myself to put my fears into words.

"It doesn't happen very often here. As you pointed out, this isn't the big city. But we don't want her wandering the streets alone, either. It'll be dark soon."

Dark and cold, I thought.

The officer wanted to search the apartment again, so we went through Brianna's few belongings. I told Officer Pat that nothing seemed to be missing except Brianna's coat. I picked up a drawing tablet that we'd given Brianna, along with some crayons. She'd promptly informed us that she was "too old" for crayons, but to my surprise, Brianna had filled the pages of the drawing tablet with quite impressive-looking renderings of flowers and gardens.

Officer Pat planted herself by the phone again while I went out to the kitchen. All I could do was pray silently over and over again: Please, Father, let Brianna be okay. I scraped the stuffing out of the turkey and put it in a Tupperware bowl in the fridge. Then I started trying to deal with the rest of the prepared dinner. I covered the pies with plastic wrap and then I went into the hallway to the drawer where we kept the tape. The tape was missing.

What would Brianna want with tape? I wondered. Paul must've left it out somewhere.

Finally, I managed to squeeze the turkey into the fridge. I put the juices into a jar for gravy. I washed the roasting pan. Then I was out of things to do, and I was beside myself. It would be dark soon. Alone in the kitchen, I started to cry. A troubled little girl had needed my help and what did she get from me?

It came to me then that Brianna kept bringing up my baby's death because she was trying to connect with me—and also because, as a ten-year-old, she was genuinely, innocently curious about the concepts of life and death. Paul and I kept acting cheerful with her, as though nothing was wrong, but things were wrong. I was grieving my baby and so was Paul. And Brianna's life was changing in a way that frightened her, and her mother had gone off somewhere with a man whom Brianna had only met a few times. Brianna felt a sense of loss, and she knew that I did, too. She'd been trying to talk with me about what mattered to us both, I realized, and I had shut her out and wanted her to be like my daydreams of Grace instead of the very real and very troubled child that she was.

Paul and some policemen came in for coffee and went out again. Paul's face was pale and drawn; I heard the words, "television alert soon," spoken; then they were gone again. Officer Pat was manning the phone; there was nothing for me to do except wait and hope that Brianna would come home soon.

It was the thought of Brianna coming home that gave me the idea. It was probably silly, I knew, so I left a note for Paul on the kitchen table, telling him where I was going, and got my coat. I quietly let myself out when Officer Pat went to the bathroom.

It was less than a mile from our place to the apartment house where Brianna used to live with Paul and her mother. Surely, somebody else was living in that apartment now, but what if Brianna had gone there? Would she even remember which apartment it was? I jogged through the dark streets, looking everywhere for her.

It was a bigger building than ours, somewhat run-down, with no doorman. I rang the buzzer for the super and was buzzed inside. There was a small, brightly lit lobby.

"What do you want?" asked a heavily accented voice from the end of the lobby. There were rich food aromas wafting through the lobby and the sound of voices coming from the super's apartment; they were having Thanksgiving dinner. The super was a middle-aged man who looked annoyed at having his holiday meal interrupted.

"My little girl is missing," I told him. "She used to live here, and I thought she might've come back." It seemed like a silly idea once I'd expressed it.

"There's no little girl here. How would she get in the building?"

"I was thinking maybe she came in when someone who lives here let themselves in."

"But there's no little girl here."

I tried to have patience. "She used to live here with her father and mother, the Marsdens."

"I remember the Marsdens," the super said with a suspicious look. "You aren't the mother."

"They're divorced. I'm Brianna's stepmother. Can you tell me what apartment they lived in?"

"They lived in 3C. But an elderly couple lives there now. They went to visit their kids for Thanksgiving. She's not here, the little girl." He promptly closed his door in my face.

I went upstairs and knocked on the door of 3C. I even tried the doorknob. I was being silly, and I knew it. I didn't want to wait for the old, slow elevator again, so I took the stairwell down. That's when I noticed that another flight went down, and it was all lit up down there, so I went on down.

The basement was brightly lit. There were several spaces sectioned off with cages for tenants to store things, all the cages were padlocked. The laundry room was empty, smelling strongly of detergent, fabric softener, and clean lint. Nobody was doing laundry on Thanksgiving. I opened a door marked Furnace, surprised to find it unlocked. A large, fairly modern-looking furnace stood inside. Beyond it was an old-fashioned coal bin that probably hadn't been used since the Forties. I could see the chute where the coal used to come into the building; the wooden walls of the bin were about five feet high and they'd long since been painted white. I wondered why they hadn't been removed, since coal bins aren't used anymore.

I walked around to an opening into the bin. Brianna was asleep on the concrete floor, using her coat as a blanket. The book I'd given her, The Secret Garden, lay nearby. On the painted walls of the coal bin, she'd taped up dozens of crayon drawings of flowers. Brianna was asleep in her secret garden.

I climbed in and knelt next to her. Relaxed in sleep, her face looked like I always imagined Grace's face would look. I realized that this was because Brianna looked like Paul. She looked so small and sweet, curled up on the floor.

I shook her gently. "Grace," I whispered. "Oh—I mean—Brianna."

"Who's Grace?" she asked sleepily, slowly sitting up.

"My baby that I lost."

"You must be so mad that Grace died and all you have is me."

I pulled her into my arms. To my surprise, she let me. "I've been very sad about Grace for a long time, Brianna. But I'm glad we have you, and I was very, very scared when I thought I'd lost you, too."

"I thought you didn't want me around."

I tipped her face up. "I want you around, Brianna. Your daddy wants you around. Get it?"

She gave me a tentative smile. It may have been the first time I ever saw her smile.

A little while later, as we came out of the building together, a patrol car pulled up at the curb out front and Paul leaped out. He raced to meet us and embraced Brianna, swinging her into his arms. He was crying and so was she. So was I.

The cops in the patrol car radioed in the good news as they drove us home. We rode in the back of the patrol car with Brianna snuggled between us.

"Happy Thanksgiving!" the cops said in unison as they dropped us off.

10

"Good heavens," Paul said as we stood on the sidewalk, "the turkey!"

I laughed. "Anyone for hot turkey sandwiches?"

It wasn't smooth sailing with Brianna from then on, but things were better. Paul and I set a policy of being honest about our feelings with her so she would always know where she stood. When she was rude, we told her it upset us. When I was sad, I said so. At the end of that visit, she hugged us good-bye.

The following year, she willingly came to stay with us for the summer. I was pregnant by then, and we knew it would be a boy. The doctor had told me that I shouldn't have any more children, so Brianna became my little girl. She's a very different little girl than I imagined, but a happy reality is always better than a daydream.

THE END

HOLIDAY TRADITIONS
Will I ever break free?

My earliest memory of Thanksgiving involved a whole week of my mother frantically rushing around cleaning, shopping, barking orders at Daddy to keep his muddy shoes off the carpet, and making us dress up in very uncomfortable clothes that we hated.

On the big day, she went into overdrive with last-minute cooking and handing me a feather duster to give all the tables a quick swipe before the guests arrived. She always looked like she was ready to blow a gasket at any time.

Once everyone arrived at our house, she wore a big smile plastered on her lips, as if everything was under control. Well, I suppose it was under her control, but we hated every minute of it. Where were the blessings we were supposed to be giving thanks for?

Sure we had plenty of food and lots of nice things, but I don't remember Thanksgiving ever being a happy time. All I remember is the stress and anxiety from having so much to do at such a busy time of year.

"Oh, Rachel," my dad's sister said as she walked through the door to our heavily decorated living room. "You do such a nice job with the holidays. How do you find the time to do all this?"

Mom acted like it was nothing. "Oh, I just throw a few things together. And the kids help."

Yeah, the kids helped. My sisters, brother, and I almost gagged when we heard Mom say that. I was the youngest of four, and from the time I could walk, I dusted, swept, and wiped things clean until I couldn't see a speck of dust or dirt anywhere. But Mom could. Most of the time she had me do it all over again.

And then there was the shopping. Mom made a new list every day. We had things that had to be prepared a week in advance, then every day after that there was something else. She made us go to the grocery store with her, something none of us liked. But she said she needed help with the baskets since she often needed more than one.

Even Daddy told her to slow down a little because our house was so frantic. "Rachel, you're killing yourself over this one day. Why don't you kick back a little and enjoy it?"

She just growled at him, saying, "If I don't do this work, then no one will have a nice Thanksgiving. It's our tradition."

I quickly grew to hate the very word "tradition." Because of what Mom had done to us kids, I associated it with all bad things that I never wanted to inflict on my family.

This continued through the years, even after my older sisters and brother moved away. Mom always beckoned them home, saying she'd make sure they had the same kind of Thanksgiving they had as children. She probably thought it was important, but I saw the guilt that kept them coming back.

"Heaven help us," my oldest sister, Alison, said when she got there. "Does she actually think she's doing us a favor by rushing around like this?"

I took her coat. "I think she enjoys it, but I still don't know what there is to like about all this."

Looking around the living room, I saw ceramic turkeys, orange and brown raffia bows, and gourds filled with fake vegetables, all strategically placed to give people the feeling they were pilgrims at the first feast. All I saw was more stuff that would have to be wrapped and put away until next year when we'd drag all this stuff back out.

"Is this still a formal sit-down affair?" my brother, Bobby, said when he guided his new wife, Courtney, through the house and toward the kitchen.

"Afraid so," I said, glancing down at the dress Mom had insisted I wear. "Look at me. I never dress like this, not even for church."

"You look miserable," Bobby said.

"Trust me, I am."

Courtney's eyes were huge as she realized she was terribly underdressed. "I didn't bring anything," she whispered loud enough for me to hear.

I took her by the arm and dragged her upstairs to my room. "C'mon, I've got something that'll probably fit." Fortunately for her, we were about the same size. Mom would've had a fit if she'd seen what she'd been wearing when they first arrived. It was a very pretty pair of cream-colored slacks and a coral sweater that looked beautiful against her skin. But it was too casual for my mother's Thanksgiving.

"Isn't that your dress, Sandra?" my mother asked when she saw what Courtney was wearing.

I nodded. "I thought it would look pretty on her," I said.

Courtney grinned and looked sheepish. "I wasn't dressed for the occasion, I'm afraid. Next time I'll know."

Instead of being gracious about it, Mom just raised her eyebrows and said, "We're creating memories here, and I expect them to be good ones. No sloppiness allowed."

I turned to Courtney and watched her cringe. Bobby literally had to hold her up.

My two sisters' families were used to this because they'd been through it a couple of times before. The only person who balked at it was Alison's husband, Ross, who told my mom she was wound too tight. I agreed with him, but I was afraid to say so. Mom never said a word back to Ross since he came from such a well-known family in town. I suppose she thought it was okay for him to voice his opinion.

Before sitting down to dinner, we always had to pose for family pictures, which would be added to the gallery on the piano. Mom even told us where to stand so the pictures would be symmetrical and we'd look our best. She never believed in acting natural and relaxing.

I don't think anyone ever had fun, with the exception of my mother, and even with her, I wasn't sure. She was so frantic and stressed, her face took on a pinched look, and her shrill voice could be heard from the driveway.

My last year of high school was a particularly difficult time for me, since I was trying to get into the best college in the state. I had more homework than ever, besides having to study for placement tests and SATs. Daddy even told Mom that I needed to concentrate on my studies rather than get involved in her holiday planning.

She just shook her head and said, "There are important things to do around here, and I don't want to have to do them all myself. We're making memories, and I'd think that would be more important to you than schoolwork that can be done afterward."

I knew better than to argue, so I just got to work with the duster. Mom was in the kitchen baking pies from scratch. Once, when Alison suggested she either get pies from the bakery or even use frozen ones, Mom just freaked.

"How can you suggest such a thing?" she said. "People have come to expect a certain quality from Thanksgiving dinner at our house, and I don't plan to disappoint them."

I even tried to talk to her one year. "I heard the grocery store is smoking turkeys and offering a package with dressing, gravy, and rolls for one set price. That way you wouldn't have to get up at four o'clock in the morning to start cooking."

"I'd never do that grocery store prepared thing," she said. "Part of the fun is getting up and sticking the turkey in the oven."

Fun? I didn't think so. So far, I'd never considered that a bit of fun. In fact, it was so tedious I wanted to run away. But I couldn't. Mom needed me, so I was there. It was a catch-22. I hated every minute of it, but I wasn't about to upset or disappoint Mom.

Immediately after dinner that year, I had to go to my room to study. I had a test on Monday, and it determined whether or not I'd be able to get into the college of my choice. I heard Mom asking Daddy where I was. I couldn't hear what he said, but she didn't come after me. It must be good, I thought, then got back to my books, blocking out the sounds of people downstairs.

14

I managed to get into the college I wanted, and I couldn't have been happier. As my parents dropped me off at my dorm room, my mom turned to me and said, "Don't forget we're having a very special Thanksgiving this year. We'll also be celebrating the new arrival of our third grandchild."

My sister was having a baby in late October, and my mom was excited to have another infant to add to the picture gallery on the piano. She said it showed family continuity. I knew it was so she could show her bridge club how close her family was, especially during the holidays. I'd even heard them remark to her that they wished their children looked so forward to coming to their house as my mom's children did. I knew it wasn't so much that as feeling guilty if they didn't.

I made it home the day before Thanksgiving. Mom handed me my traditional feather duster and gave me very strict instructions of what to dust and then what to do afterward. Most of the housework that she should've done days before hadn't been touched. That surprised me. Mom was always so particular about things and so organized, too. When I completed my chores, I went to the kitchen to help her. I was shocked to see how much was left undone.

"I don't know what's going on," she said as she stood in front of the stove fanning something that had burned. "It's not like I'm doing anything I didn't used to do. But it does seem like more."

"Mom, maybe it's time you slowed down a little," I said. For the first time in my life I saw how my mom had aged. And it had only been three months since I'd last seen her.

"Never," she said as she turned back to the stove. "As long as I'm capable, we'll continue on in the family tradition."

I let out a long sigh and shook my head. Now I knew it was just plain stubbornness that kept her going. And maybe a little pride, too. It was clear to me that Mom didn't like doing this anymore.

"Maybe you can talk to her," I told Alison, who was also concerned. "She looked downright frazzled when I got home. And the meal isn't anywhere near done."

Alison shrugged out of her coat. "As much as I hate to say this, we need to back off and let Mom decide when to slow down. We can talk till we're blue in the face, but she's not gonna listen."

"You're probably right, but I don't like watching her fall apart."

Suddenly, Mom's shrill scream brought all of us into the kitchen. Alison grabbed the flaming oven mitt from Mom and tossed it into the sink. Then she pointed her finger and ordered Mom out of the kitchen until she and I could get things cleaned up.

"See?" I said. "We can't wait for her to decide. We have to do something."

"Yeah, you're probably right," she agreed. "Let me think about how to go about it. In the meantime, hand me that dishrag over there."

The two of us cleaned the kitchen and got things going again. We'd been through enough Thanksgivings with Mom that we knew exactly what to do. It took us all day to get caught up, but we managed with both of us working.

Dad came in and told us Mom was taking a nap. "She's sleeping," he said. "Don't wake her."

Alison glanced over at me, and then she turned to Dad. "We need to talk, Dad."

I backed toward the stairs. "Let me go check on everyone to make sure they have everything they need. Be right back."

Alison's family had all gone upstairs to their room to freshen up. The rest of our family hadn't yet arrived, and I was glad.

Once I knew Alison's husband and kids were all taken care of, I went back downstairs where Alison and Dad were already deep in conversation. I caught the tail end of something about how Mom hadn't been herself lately.

"What's going on with her?" I asked.

"I don't know, but she has a doctor's appointment next week," he told us.

"Any idea what it could be?" Alison asked.

"No idea whatsoever, but I'll let both of you know as soon as we find out."

That Thanksgiving started out like all the others, with Mom getting up early and barking orders. Then an hour before we were to sit down and eat, she went upstairs to get "freshened up," which was another way of saying bathed, dressed, and fully made up. It took her a little longer than usual, but when she finally descended the stairs she looked as beautiful as ever.

Alison and I stuck close by Mom's side while she did her usual thing. Both of us noticed her slight tremor as she carried plates to the dining room.

"Here, Mom, let me do that," Alison said, literally yanking some utensils from her hand.

There were a few times when Mom actually looked lost in her own kitchen. My heart ached at the thought of Mom aging, but I knew it would happen one of these days.

Thanksgiving went okay, but if it weren't for Alison and me, there would have been some problems. Dad insisted on Mom going upstairs to rest before she started cleaning up. Then Elaine, my other sister, my sister-in-law, and I got right to work, washing dishes, cleaning pots and pans, and vacuuming floors. By the time Mom came back downstairs most of the work was done.

16

"Oh my, you shouldn't have," she said. "But there's still a lot that needs to be done." Mom went back into overdrive, cleaning things that didn't need it.

Alison just shrugged and took a step back. "She needs to feel needed," she explained. "But next year I'm having Thanksgiving at my house."

"Are you sure?" I asked.

"Positive," she stated firmly. "I can't go through this again."

To our surprise, Mom didn't argue. She just said, "I hope you remember all the things I taught you. Having a memorable Thanksgiving requires a lot of preparation and hard work."

"Yes, I know, Mom," Alison told her. "Sandra promised to help make sure everything goes right."

"I did?" I asked before I caught her warning glance. "Oh, yeah, I did."

"Just don't forget how much everyone appreciates everything made from scratch." She leveled us both with a warning gaze. "Including the pies and turkey. I don't want to catch you doing one of those store-smoked turkeys. It can't be nearly as good."

"Okay, Mom," Alison said as she rolled her eyes.

"And the pies all have to be made from scratch, including the crust. That's the most important part."

Alison nodded. "I hear ya, Mom."

"Want to borrow my ceramic turkeys and the rest of the decorations?"

"Whatever," Alison said, knowing it wouldn't do any good to turn my mom down.

"I'll gather it all up for you before you leave," Mom said. "If you'd like for me to, I can come early and give you a hand with all the details."

A little too quickly, Alison said, "No, Mom, that won't be necessary." I almost burst out laughing. We were talking about a holiday that was a whole year away.

As soon as I had Alison to myself, I turned to her and shook my head. "You need to have your head examined."

"What?" she said. "I'm just trying to save Mom the trouble."

"I can't believe all the things she made you promise."

"You expect me to keep those promises?" she said.

"You'd better. Mom will know the difference."

"We'll see," she said with a sly grin.

I was relieved when Dad called me at college and told me that Mom's physical problem was only exhaustion. "She's stressed over all the things she feels she needs to do," he said wearily.

"I hope you make her slow down," I advised.

"I'm doing my best, but you know your mother."

The very next Thanksgiving was almost a total disaster. Alison tried to get away with hiding the bakery boxes and the package the turkey came in. Mom could tell the difference—that Alison had bought everything already prepared. And for that matter, so could I.

It wouldn't have mattered to me, though, but with Mom raising such a ruckus, this was the most stressful Thanksgiving ever. I wanted it the way it was before, even if it meant going to Alison's house and doing most of the work myself.

"Okay, okay," Alison said when it was all over. "Next year I'll do it your way, Mom."

"If you don't, then we're having it back at my house," Mom said in a tone that let us know she wasn't kidding around.

"Is she trying to threaten me?" Alison said when Mom went upstairs for her nap. "She's the one who needs to be grateful."

"I know, but she's pretty stubborn," I said.

The rest of our siblings didn't really care what we ate, what time we ate, or how the house was decorated. I have to admit, I liked the festive atmosphere, but I did think Mom carried it too far.

Alison, on the other hand, was a people pleaser. She wanted everyone to have a good time and to go away happy and full.

The Thanksgiving after that was almost an exact replica of Mom's. "You did a great job, Alison," I told her. "Mom's really proud of you."

"Yeah," she said with exhaustion written all over her face. "But I could sleep for ten years and never wake up."

I laughed. "Don't even think about doing something like that. You have to at least wait until I'm out of college. Then you and I can take turns having Thanksgiving at our houses."

"Sounds good," she said.

Mom was relentless with her tradition. No matter how much work it took or how busy we were during that time of year, she insisted on everything being done her way. No shortcuts. Nothing could be dropped. We had to have all the decorations and food exactly like she'd always done it.

"Just once," Alison said, "I'd like to have a casual buffet dinner. I've had it with the sit-down meal where I feel like a slave." She said this the day after the second Thanksgiving at her house.

"You've only done this twice, Alison. Mom did it for twenty-something years."

"Yeah, I know, but it's still pretty ridiculous."

"Then why don't you change the tradition?" I asked.

"You know Mom."

"Yeah," I said. "I know Mom. She'll have a hissy fit and

probably insist on taking it back to her house, but we can stand firm as long as we're united."

"No," Alison finally said. "I don't want to upset her. She hasn't exactly been healthy lately, in case you haven't noticed."

I let out a sigh. "Yeah, I know that. But maybe she'll see where we can have more fun if we let loose and just have a good time."

"Tell you what, Sandra. When you have your own house and you take your turn, then experiment all you want. I tried doing things differently once, and look what happened."

I had two more years of college since I'd changed my major so many times. During my second to last semester, I met Joey, an accounting major. He was very sweet, which was the reason I fell in love with him. My parents liked him because he had a bright future ahead of him and he was very family oriented.

Joey loved the fact that my family had traditions. I'd told him about it and probably glamorized it a little. When I told him we carried it a little too far, he shook his head. "Family traditions are important in this day and age. Too many people have gotten away from them, and look where we're headed."

Since Joey and I lived in a tiny apartment, we had one more year of Thanksgiving at Alison's house. I watched Joey's face as he saw everything unfold.

"I see what you're saying, Sandra," Joey told me when it was over. "Your mom takes the tradition thing a little too seriously. I've never been so uncomfortable at a family dinner in my entire life. It's more like a business dinner."

He loosened his tie and undid the top button on his dress shirt. I kicked off my dress shoes and tugged my pantyhose off in the car on the way home.

"Next year, hopefully, we'll have a bigger place. Then we'll show your family how to have a really fun Thanksgiving," he said.

"Everyone in my family will love it, except my mom," I told him. "She's the one you'll have to convince."

"Trust me," he said. "I'll have her eating out of my hand by the end of the day." He squeezed my hand and added, "We'll have a nice, relaxing day."

"Thanksgiving should be a time of joy and family togetherness," I said. "Not stress. I don't remember ever feeling relaxed at that time of year."

"Leave it up to me next year," he said. "If she gets upset, I'll take the blame."

Joey got a bonus from work six months later, so we used it to put a down payment on a house and we got married. "Now we can have Thanksgiving at our house," he said.

19

"You sure you wanna do that?" I asked. "Mom will expect everything to be just so."

"Yes, and it will be," he assured me. "It will be just so, according to the tradition we're about to start."

I worried that if Mom got upset over the differences, which I was certain there would be, she'd never want to have Thanksgiving with us again.

When I told everyone in my family we were holding the celebration at our house, they were all excited. Alison sounded thrilled about it.

"Joey is such a nice guy to be willing to do this. Does he know how persnickety Mom is?"

"Yes, I told him, but he's willing to stick his neck out and do things his own way."

Alison laughed. "Let's hope he gets away with it. Care to place a bet?"

"No," I told her. "Mom's pretty adamant about the way things have to be done, and I refuse to bet against my husband."

"If anyone can pull it off, I suspect he can," Alison said. "We all really like him, especially Mom."

I had noticed that Mom took an instant liking to Joey. In fact, he'd turned his charm on her, and I caught her grinning and laughing in a way I'd never seen her do before. Perhaps Alison was right. Maybe he could pull it off.

When the weather started cooling off, I reminded Joey of our offer to have Thanksgiving dinner at our house. He nodded and said he had everything under control and to leave it up to him.

"But I need to know what to cook," I told him. "And a shopping list."

"Don't worry, Sandra. I'll take care of everything."

After a big sigh, I said, "Then we'll have to start cleaning early. Mom likes everything shiny and bright."

"That's taken care of, too," he said as he hugged me. "Relax, okay? I don't want you to stress over this like you used to."

"I'll try."

I had no idea what Joey was up to, but he seemed so sure about the whole thing. He wasn't worried in the least.

A week before Thanksgiving, I reminded him that we needed to do some shopping. "I'll give you a list on Tuesday," he said.

"The turkey won't have time to thaw by Thursday."

"We're not getting a frozen turkey."

Naturally, since he said that, I assumed we were getting a fresh turkey on Wednesday. But I still needed to know what was expected of me.

"Absolutely nothing, Sandra," Joey said as he kissed me on the cheek. "I refuse to keep up the tradition of stressing the people I love. I love you, and I want you to enjoy the holiday, not dread it."

On Tuesday, Joey handed me a very short list of items we needed at the grocery store. "That's all?" I asked. "How are we gonna come up with a dinner for my whole family from the stuff on here? Mom used to go to the store every day for a week and each time fill a couple baskets."

Joey sighed, shook his head, and chuckled. "You worry way too much. Just trust me."

I got the things on his list, but I had to admit, I was still worried. It seemed almost wrong not to be fretting over all the tiny details this close to Thanksgiving.

When I got home, Joey was on the phone with my mom. For the first time since he'd offered our home for the holiday, he looked worried.

"You wanna talk to her?" he mouthed.

I nodded. The minute I took the phone, I felt an overwhelming sense of dread. My mom was crying, saying there was no way she could participate in the travesty of this special holiday.

"I simply can't believe you'd go this far," she said between sobs.

My dad grabbed the phone from her and promised he'd continue working on her but he couldn't promise anything. I thanked him before hanging up.

When I turned to Joey, he was staring down at the floor, deep in thought. Finally, he grabbed his car keys, headed for the door, and said, "I'll be back. I'm going to visit your folks."

He came back home around midnight saying everything was under control. "Your mom said she'd come but not to expect her to like any of it," he told me. "We'll just have to make sure she has a good time."

"What happened?" I asked.

"I told her things would be a little different this year," he said.

"Oh, man. Exactly what did she say about that?"

He shook his head. "You don't wanna know."

On Wednesday I had to work an hour late since the long weekend was coming up. Joey told me he'd be home early, so he'd make sure everything was done at home. At this point, I had no choice but to trust Joey, who'd promised me we'd have the best Thanksgiving ever.

When I got home, my entire house was sparkling clean. Joey had carefully placed Mom's decorations around the house, making it look as festive as it always had. Only this year, I hadn't had to lift a finger. He even added some candles in strategic places, which made the house look even prettier.

I praised him for all he'd done in such a short time. He chuckled. "I hired a cleaning service. As soon as they were done, I spent every bit of an hour decorating."

"That's all?" I said. "Looks to me like you've been working on this all week."

"That's the beauty of hiring a cleaning service. They come in with a crew and they're out in an hour."

I had to admit, they did as good a job as I've ever done. Mom couldn't complain about the place not being up to her standards.

"What about the food?" I asked.

He glanced at his watch. "I'm picking it up in fifteen minutes."

"Picking it up?" I said. Now I knew we were in trouble. Mom liked her turkey and dressing cooked a specific way, and she wouldn't accept anything else.

"Yeah, I gave the recipe for the dressing to a caterer my company uses for special occasions, and they gave me a cut price if I pick it up rather than have them deliver it."

"I hope you know what you're doing," I said.

"Like I said before, Sandra, you just have to trust me." He paused before adding, "I just hope your mom has an open mind about this. She's the only one I'm worried about."

My mom was the only one any of us had been worried about all this time. If it weren't for her, I knew we'd have done away with the formal dinner and the stress a long time ago. Alison had even said she was tempted to eat out for Thanksgiving rather than have to face this another year.

By the time we went to bed on Wednesday, our refrigerator was filled with food for our meal the next day. All we had to do was heat up a few things, and we'd have Thanksgiving dinner. When I took a quick peek at the dressing, I noticed it looked identical to Mom's. Maybe she wouldn't notice it wasn't homemade.

Early Thursday morning, Joey got up and started rummaging around in the garage. "What're you doing in there?" I asked as I stood by the door wearing my robe and slippers.

"Looking for the croquet set."

When we first bought the house, Joey's parents let us have the family croquet set and the badminton net that had been in his family for years. The badminton net was already set up in our backyard from the weekend before when the neighbors came over for a cookout.

"Why do you need the croquet set?" I asked.

"So we can have some fun before dinner."

He said that like I should've already known. I just shrugged and went back inside. It would take me a while to get ready for my family, and I hadn't even picked out a dress to wear yet.

22

"Oh," Joey told me when he came back inside the house. "You don't have to get too dressed up. I already called everyone in your family and told them we were going casual this year."

I gasped. "How can you do that? You know how my mom is."

He shrugged. "They didn't seem to mind. In fact, they sounded pretty pleased about it."

"But my mom—" I was beginning to sound like a broken record.

"Your mom will be fine once she realizes we're not trying to sabotage her perfect holiday. We're only trying to improve on what she started."

"She won't like this a single bit," I warned.

"Look, Sandra, we're using her decorations, her recipes, and the house is spotless. The only thing we're changing is the way people dress."

"Okay, don't say I didn't warn you."

Bobby and his family were the first to arrive. I gasped when I saw what they were wearing. "Mom will have a heart attack when she sees you," I told Bobby. He had on jeans and a polo shirt, rather than his usual suit and tie.

He grinned as he bent over and kissed me on the cheek. "You worry too much, Sandra. Mom will get over it, and we might have a good time for a change."

Then my sister, Phoebe, came. She was wearing a nice pair of slacks and a sweater. At least she wasn't as casual as Bobby.

"I brought a change of clothes, just in case," she whispered as she walked by me.

"Oh, good, a dress." At least she could make a quick change if Mom was mad.

"No, jeans. Joey told us we were playing backyard games. I don't want to mess up these good clothes."

Then Alison's family came in their casual clothes. By the time I saw them, I'd expected it.

My heart sank. While my sisters and brother were all happy about being comfortable, I knew my mom would be furious. She'd consider this a mockery of her favorite holiday.

I kept watching out the window nervously for my parents. When I finally spotted their car pulling up the street, I began to tremble.

I stood at the front window, waiting. First my dad got out, and I was shocked to see that he was wearing khaki pants and a polo shirt. How'd he get away with leaving the house like that, I wondered. Then he went around and opened the door for Mom.

When she stepped out of the car, I almost fainted. She was wearing black slacks and a silk shell with a matching jacket loosely hanging around her shoulders.

I spun around to see Joey standing behind me wearing a grin. "What did you say to them about what to wear?" I asked.

He shrugged. "I just told them to come casual because we were starting a new tradition." After clearing his throat, he added, "But I have to admit, I wasn't sure they'd actually do it."

I knew there had to be more to it than that, but I didn't say anything. I just went to the door and greeted my mom and dad, who looked as uncomfortable as I felt.

"This is silly, if you ask me," Mom said. "How can we call this a special occasion dressed like this?"

Now I knew she was miserable, which let me know that some things hadn't changed—and probably never would. Apparently, my dad had talked her into wearing slacks rather than a dress, and she didn't like it a bit. I knew that Joey didn't have the power to change my mom after all those years of her traditional dressy Thanksgivings.

Once everyone was in the house, Joey directed them all to the backyard. It was a cool, crisp November day that was perfect for outdoor games. Joey had already set up the croquet set on one side of the yard, and the badminton set was beckoning the more active of the group. Somehow, Joey had come up with a horseshoe set in another part of the yard. My dad's eyes lit up.

"Horseshoes," he said. "I haven't played that in years. C'mon, Joey, I challenge you to a game."

Joey had his camera out, and he snapped a few pictures before he nodded to my dad and said, "You're on."

Almost immediately, everyone was involved in one game or another, and they all seemed to be having fun. Everyone, that is, but my mom. She just stood on the back porch, watching, tears misting her eyes.

At some point, I saw a change come over my mom, and it seemed to bring overwhelming sadness to her. It broke my heart to see her like this.

"Mom," I said. "I can go change if you want me to."

She reached out her hand to me and shook her head. "No, Sandra, stay just like you are. It's just hard for me to watch all this, knowing your father was right and I was wrong."

"Right and wrong about what?" I asked.

"For years your father told me I needed to relax more and just let people be themselves on Thanksgiving. I insisted on doing everything the exact same way because I always thought that tradition was important."

"It is," I told her.

"Yes, but that doesn't mean it has to be stuffy. I noticed all the decorations in your house, set up just like I would have."

I nodded. "The house has always been beautiful for the holidays."

"Your house is spotless, too, just like our house was when you were growing up. You must have spent days cleaning."

I didn't say a word. No sense in telling Mom about the fact that Joey had splurged and hired a cleaning service.

When it was time to eat, Joey rounded everyone up and herded them into the kitchen. "This is buffet style, so help yourself," he told them.

Since Joey had organized this, he told me to let him put the finishing touches on the meal. I had no idea he'd planned to do the dinner buffet style. I gasped. But when I glanced around the room, I saw people nodding—with the exception of my mom, who stood at the door looking dumbfounded.

The kitchen was noisy and crowded as people heaped mashed potatoes and turkey on their plates. Eventually, Mom got into the spirit as she fixed her own plate. She even cracked a smile at a comment Joey made about slaving over the hot stove all day. I stood back in amazement over the whole thing.

Bobby led the blessing, and then we all sat down to eat—adults in the dining room and children in the kitchen. Joey made the announcement that we'd have Thanksgiving at our house again next year, and he'd make sure we had a picnic table in case someone wanted to eat outside. That brought a cheer from the kids and Bobby, who I suspected would always be a kid at heart. Alison sighed with relief. Mom's mouth flew open, but then she closed it and slowly nodded. It choked me up watching the realization dawn on her that this was the most fun anyone had ever had.

Everyone helped clean up afterward, and the kitchen was spotless in record time. My mom came up from behind me and whispered, "The dressing was exactly like mine. You and Joey did an excellent job with dinner."

I didn't tell her it was catered. I just smiled and thanked her.

Once all the work was done, the kids were set up in the kitchen with children's board games, and the adults went into the living room for a game of charades—men on one team and women on the other. The women beat the guys pretty badly, and we all laughed so hard we had tears streaming down our cheeks.

When it was time for everyone to leave, they all whispered to Joey and me that this was the best Thanksgiving they'd ever had. Mom lingered behind to talk with us.

As soon as everyone else was gone, she turned to me with tears in her eyes. She took hold of both of my hands. "Sandra, you've managed to keep most of my traditions, yet it seemed so different. I'll have to admit, I was appalled at the fact that this would be a casual affair. But your father told me to humor you and Joey. I know he's wanted to do this for a long time but he didn't want to upset me."

"None of us did, Mom," I admitted.

"I know. But I want you to know that this has been the best Thanksgiving I can ever remember. You two did a fabulous job."

Joey stood behind me with a grin and a look of relief on his face. My dad came out from behind Mom and shook Joey's hand. "Good job, son," my dad said. Joey beamed.

Once they were gone, I turned to my husband and hugged him. "I'm so proud of you, Joey."

He seemed uncomfortable with all the praise that had been heaped on him. He hugged me back, and then squirmed away from me. "Oh, I got some great pictures. I'll have copies made for everyone so they won't forget the day."

Grinning back at him, I said, "Trust me, Joey, they'll never forget this day. It was the best Thanksgiving ever."

THE END

THE CLOWN PRINCE
This Is The Start Of A New Thanksgiving Tradition.

It was a week before Thanksgiving, and I was over a thousand miles away from home. It would be the first time in my life that I wouldn't be with my family for the holiday. I thought about all the things I would miss, like Dad carving the turkey, Mom's pumpkin pie, and Aunt Cara's fruit salad. My sister Miranda would be there with her husband Jim and their two little girls. Uncle Bud would entertain everyone with his card tricks, and all that would be going on while I was far away in Mayfield.

Six months earlier, I had moved to Mayfield to take my dream job. When I arrived, I thought the area, with its tall trees and rolling hills, was the most beautiful place I had ever seen. Ordinarily, I wouldn't have complained. I loved my job. Part writer, part graphic designer, I was in charge of producing the catalogs for a large mail-order company with its headquarters in Mayfield. The problem was that when I wasn't working, I didn't know what to do with myself.

I liked my co-workers, especially my assistant Shirley. But everyone I worked with had a family and a life outside the office that didn't leave much time for socialization after work. I hadn't made any friends outside my job either, and in the entire time I'd been there, I hadn't met anyone I wanted to go out with.

So I went to work and listened politely while my co-workers made their plans for Thanksgiving. I nodded when they discussed their menus, and I sympathized when they complained about how much work their festivities would be. I even laughed as they described the antics of their various family members. How I envied them.

"What about you, Abbie?" a woman in my department asked me. "What are you doing for Thanksgiving?"

"I haven't decided yet," I told her. "I have several options."

Luckily she didn't ask what my options were. One option would be to go by a deli and pick up a small, ready-made turkey dinner. Another option would be to pick up a frozen dinner and heat it up in the oven. Both of those options involved watching television with my meal. I wouldn't consider going to a restaurant, where I would have to eat alone, while everyone at the nearby tables felt sorry for me.

The last option would be to stay in bed and sleep through Thanksgiving entirely. I confess I'd been leaning toward that idea.

I didn't want my co-workers to know that I would be spending the holiday alone, because I didn't want anyone to invite me to join them out of pity.

On Friday night, my sister Melanie called for her weekly chat. During the conversation, she gave me some unexpected news.

"Have you heard that Angus' new wife is expecting?" she asked.

Angus was my ex-boyfriend. We hadn't parted on good terms, and I didn't really care what his wife did. But at that moment, hearing that she was pregnant made me feel even more homesick. I told my sister that I hadn't heard about it and changed the subject.

I had dated Angus for almost two years, and during that time, he had constantly tried to boss me around.

"Is that what you're going to wear?" he used to ask. Or, "Don't you think you should get to work a little earlier in the morning? It would make a better impression on your boss."

Then, if I left for work earlier, Angus would say, "What's your hurry? You're just going to work."

He hated the job I had back then, because I had to travel.

"You're always out of town," he complained over and over.

I tried to reason with him. "Angus, I go out of town once a month, and I'm only gone one night."

But it didn't do any good. He wouldn't listen to reason. Every time I went out of town, he threw a fit.

"I want you home with me," he insisted. "Get another job, one that only requires you to work forty hours a week, with no overtime and no travel."

I had laughed. "Maybe I could find a job where I only had to work an hour a day with an hour off for lunch."

Angus wasn't amused. "When we get married, you can quit your job and be a full-time wife."

Surprised, I'd asked, "Can I? Does that mean you're proposing?"

"Uh, I don't know," he'd mumble.

His attitude had irritated me. He hadn't proposed, but he had assumed that I would marry him. And he thought that if we did get married, he could tell me what to do. Well I had no intention of marrying him, and even if I did get married to someone someday, I planned to keep my job, just like my mother had done.

Finally, Angus had given me an ultimatum. "It's me or your job."

He looked very satisfied when he said those words, but his expression changed when I answered, "No, Angus. I'm keeping my job. You want someone you can control. It isn't me. I'm not stupid enough to mistake control for love. Goodbye, Angus."

"You'll be sorry, Abbie, You'll miss me," he shouted. He was wrong.

Mom called on Saturday. "Do you have any plans for the holiday?"

28

"I thought I'd get a turkey TV dinner," I told her. "While I'm eating, I could watch the football game."

"You don't like football," she reminded me. "Haven't any of your friends invited you to dinner?"

"I don't have any friends, Mom," I whined. "The only people I know here are the people I work with, and I don't want to impose on any of them. I don't want them to invite me to dinner just because they feel sorry for me. How pathetic is that?"

"Pretty pathetic," she agreed. "Listen, Abbie, if you want to get to know people, you have to go where people are. Take a class. Join some groups. Volunteer. You shouldn't be sitting home alone."

I agreed and promised her that I would do something constructive with my time.

When I arrived at work on Monday morning, I heard Shirley talking to one of the women in our department.

"I don't know what I'm going to do, Dina," she was saying. "My husband and I always volunteer at the children's hospital on Thanksgiving. But this year, my grandmother is really sick, and my family is afraid that this will be her last Thanksgiving. So we have to spend the holiday with my family. My husband already found someone to replace him, and I have to find someone to replace me. I can't leave the other volunteers at the hospital in the lurch."

My mother's advice must have made an impression on me, because after she had finished talking to Dina, I walked up and said, "I heard you say you need someone to replace you at the children's hospital on Thanksgiving. I'll do it."

Relief flooded her face. "Really? But Abbie, I thought you had plans."

"I do, but none of them seem as interesting or as important as working at the hospital," I assured her. "I'll be happy to do this for you."

"Thank you so much," Shirley gushed. "You don't know what a favor you'll be doing me."

"I'm sorry about your grandmother," I said.

Shirley nodded. "So am I, but hopefully she'll rally and be all right."

"What will I be doing at the hospital? Working with the children?"

She grinned. "Not exactly. You'll be working for the children and having a lot of fun assisting the magician with his act. I'll have Wilson Mitchell pick you up. He's the magician."

Wilson Mitchell, my mind repeated the name. There was something about the name that seemed familiar, like I'd heard it before, but I was sure I never had. I wondered what he looked like.

For the rest of that week, I found myself looking forward to my unexpected Thanksgiving plans.

That feeling evaporated when Wilson Mitchell knocked on my door. The man was dressed as a clown. He wore a garish red and gold jumpsuit, and he had painted his face with white greasepaint and put on a big red nose. A shocking orange wig covered the top of his head.

"Wilson Mitchell?" I asked tentatively as I opened the door.

"That's me," he said. "But today you can call me Norbert the clown. Are you Abbie Rourke?" When I nodded, he asked, "Are you ready?"

"I thought you were a magician," I said.

His smile added to the grin painted on his face. "I am. I do funny magic."

I wondered what that was.

I followed him out to his car where he moved a large pair of shoes off the passenger seat. "My clown shoes," he explained. "I can't drive in them."

"How long have you been doing funny magic at the hospital?" I asked as he pulled away from the curb.

"This will be my fifth Thanksgiving."

"Should we have practiced your act?"

He shook his head, making his orange curls dance. "No. It's funnier if you don't know what to expect. Don't worry. I won't be doing anything that could frighten or embarrass you. We'll be performing three shows, one for the kids in the burn unit, one for the kids in the cancer ward, and one for all the rest of the kids. The kids in the burn unit and the cancer ward can't join the other kids in the dining room. That's why we do three shows."

"Well, I've never done anything like this before, but I'll do my best."

"Abbie, there's one thing you should know," he said slowly. "Sometimes the kids in the burn unit have horrific injuries. You might be shocked, but it's important that you don't show it. If you do, it will hurt their feelings."

"I promise that no matter what, I'll keep a straight face," I said solemnly.

"Good. Now I'm going to let you in on a secret. The Thanksgiving dinner served at the children's hospital is the best in town. You'll be enjoying a meal cooked by the head chef at the Mayfield Hotel. He volunteers to cook for the hospital on Thanksgiving."

"I didn't know we would be eating there," I admitted.

"You won't just be eating. You'll be dining. You'll see. I think half of the volunteers come just for the food."

Before I could ask if that was why he came, he pulled up in the parking lot of the hotel. "Wait just a minute so I can put my big shoes on," he said. "Then we'll go in and I'll introduce you to everyone." He tied his big shoes, picked up a canvas bag from the backseat, and we walked to the door of the hospital.

Just inside the door, a man and woman greeted us.

"Mr. and Mrs. Tyson," Wilson said, "I would like you to meet Abbie Rourke. Abbie, this is Murray and Chrissy."

"Hello, Abbie. We're glad you could volunteer today," Chrissy said as she shook my hand. "Shirley speaks highly of you."

"Thank you, Chrissy. Shirley and I work together." I looked around the hospital and noticed a lot of people milling around. "It looks like you've got a lot of volunteers today."

"We always do," Murray said. "Half of Mayfield generally turns out to help us give the kids a good Thanksgiving."

Wilson chuckled as he led me down the hall. "As I said, the kids are only one reason everyone volunteers on Thanksgiving. The other reason is the meal. But you'll see. By the way, when we're in front of the kids, please call me Norbert."

"I will, Norbert," I assured him.

As we walked down the halls of the hospital, it seemed like Wilson stopped every few steps to introduce me to someone. I met so many people that my head was spinning, and I wondered if I would be expected to remember all of their names.

Finally, Wilson hesitated in front of a pair of double doors. "Abbie, this is the burn unit. Remember what I said? Are you ready to go in?"

"Don't worry, Norbert," I said. "I won't let you down."

He stared at me for a moment. "No, I don't think you will."

Two boys were waiting when he opened the door. "It's Norbert the clown!" one of them cried out.

I had imagined the burn unit like a giant room with beds lined up along the walls. It wasn't like that at all. Instead, it was a long hall, with hospital rooms on both sides. The children were waiting for us in a large sunroom down at the end of the hall.

On the way, we passed an alcove with a large door and a sign that read, "Intensive Care. Authorized Personnel Only."

One of the boys who had been walking along beside us had a partially bandaged face. He saw me looking at the sign and said, "I used to be in there, but I'm better now.

The other boy had bandages on his arms and hands. "Roger," he indicated his friend, "was in a 'splosion. I was playing with matches. I started a fire."

Surprised by his confession, I didn't know that to say. Luckily, I didn't have to say anything, because right then, we arrived at the sunroom.

Wilson tripped over his big clown shoes as we walked in, and everyone laughed.

"Ladies and gentlemen, boys and girls, this is my beautiful assistant Abbie," Wilson announced.

"Hi, Abbie," everyone said.

Norbert the clown bent over to kiss my hand and got a violent case of the hiccups. Each time he made a noise he hopped around. With each hop, the laughter grew louder.

The large room was surrounded on three sides with windows. Chairs, filled with children of all ages, had been arranged in a semi-circle. Many of the chairs were also filled with parents, hospital staff, and volunteers.

Some of the children were heavily bandaged, and, as Wilson had warned, some of them had terrible scars. But all of them were smiling.

As I looked around the room, tears threatened my eyes, but I blinked them away and smiled back at the children.

Norbert pulled three red balls from his bag and handed them to me. "Abbie, if you'll please toss me these balls, I'll show you how to juggle."

I threw the balls to him one by one. Each time, he made a show of trying to catch the ball, but he missed all three.

"Shucks, there must be a hole in my hand," Norbert said. He held up one hand, and it actually looked like he had a hole through the center of the palm.

Everyone laughed, and one little boy scrambled to retrieve the balls. "Here, Norbert," the boy said.

Norbert took the balls from him and began to juggle them so fast that my eyes could barely keep up. Suddenly, his hands stopped, and one by one, the balls bounced off the top of his head.

Everyone laughed again.

"For my next trick, I will pull a rabbit out of a hat," the clown announced. Then he looked sheepish. "No that's wrong. I can't use a hat. I don't have one." He shrugged. "I guess I'll use a sack. But first, I want you to know that there's nothing up my sleeve." He jerked at one of the sleeves of his jumpsuit, and the sleeve came off in his hand. The kids loved it.

Then he reached into his bag and pulled out a grocery sack and a stuffed rabbit. Holding the sack open so everyone could see inside, he said, "Nothing in the sack." Then he placed the rabbit inside and set the sack on the floor.

"Abbracadabra," he said and waved his hands.

Suddenly, the paper started to move as if there really was a rabbit jumping around inside. Norbert reached into the sack and pulled out a stuffed dog.

"Rex, I wondered where you went." He looked at the audience.

"This is Rex, my dog. I couldn't find him. I thought he ran away, but all the time, he was hiding in this sack. Abbie, would you please hold Rex for me?" He handed me the dog. Then he held up the paper bag so that the audience could see that the stuffed rabbit was gone.

"For my next trick," Norbert announced, "I'm going to teach Rex to bark. That way if I can't find him, he can bark to let me know where he is. Abbracadabra." He waved his hands in front of the dog.

As I held him, Rex began to open and close his mouth while Norbert barked. I couldn't keep from laughing at that one.

Norbert's magic act went on for another twenty minutes. Part magic, part slapstick comedy, the act had everyone roaring with laughter.

Afterward, Norbert walked around the room, shaking hands with the audience and passing out candy to the children.

Several of the children came up and hugged me. "Thank you for coming, Abbie," one little girl said.

"Thank you for having me," I answered.

"You're an excellent assistant," Wilson told me after we left the burn unit. "Just as you promised, you kept a straight face. And you were as surprised as the children when I put a rabbit into a sack and pulled out a dog."

"How did you do that?" I asked.

Wilson gave a silly hop. "A magician never tells his secrets."

We repeated our performance in the cancer ward. Once again, I watched him put a rabbit into a paper bag and pull out a dog. Although I was watching closely, I still couldn't figure out how he did it.

The children were as fascinated as I was. Norbert the clown made them forget that they were injured or sick. Watching them, I realized that his comedy gave them hope.

After we left the cancer ward, I mentioned that to Wilson. "I think that just watching you makes the children feel better."

"Haven't you heard that laughter is the best medicine?" he asked.

"Yes, but this is the first time I've ever seen it in action. What's next?"

"Next is Thanksgiving dinner, that is if you don't mind eating with a clown."

"I love clowns," I told him. "Especially Norbert." Those words escaped from my lips before I realized how they would sound, and suddenly I felt uncomfortable.

But Wilson gave me a crazy bow. "And Norbert loves you too," he said.

Thanksgiving dinner was served in the hospital cafeteria, and Wilson hadn't exaggerated how good it was. I took one bite and forgot all about my parents' meal.

"Did I lie?" Wilson asked.

"Not at all," I admitted. "If anything, it's even better than you said. This is the best stuffing I've ever tasted."

"Shirley told me you worked with her on the catalog. In fact, she said you were her boss."

"Well, to tell you the truth, Shirley doesn't need any bossing. She knows almost as much about the job as I do. Tell me about yourself. What do you do when you're not clowning around?"

"I'm a doctor," Wilson told me. "I work in the emergency room at the county hospital."

"What made you start entertaining the children?"

He looked down at his plate for a moment. "Well, I've always loved to clown around, and when I was a child, I had a heart problem. It's gone now, but at that time, I spent many holidays in the hospital. I remember what it was like. Even though my parents were there, I always felt cold and lonely. So I decided that maybe I could change that for these children. One day I put on a clown suit, and here I am."

"Why magic?"

He looked up right into my eyes. His nose was red, and his hair was orange, but his eyes were the clearest gray I'd ever seen. "Magic is my hobby. When I was young, I couldn't play sports because of my heart. So one year, Dad gave me a magic set for my birthday. That was the beginning. I've been doing it ever since."

"What else can you do besides pull a stuffed dog out of a sack?"

"I can give you back the watch you lost," he said and turned over his hand. My watch was lying in his palm.

I glanced down at my empty wrist. "Wow. I didn't even know my watch was gone. How did you do that?"

"A magician never tells," he reminded me.

"Do you have any other tricks up your sleeve?" Then I remembered he didn't have any sleeves. He'd taken the other one off in the cancer ward.

We both laughed.

"Maybe I'll make you disappear," he said.

"How could you do that?" I wondered. "You don't have a cabinet in your bag of tricks."

His eyes caught mine. "You'd be surprised by what you could find in my bag of tricks."

After dinner, we did the last show in the cafeteria. Norbert tripped, juggled, and once again, he pulled a stuffed dog from a sack where a stuffed rabbit had gone in.

"Now, for the grand finale," Norbert announced, "I'm going to make my beautiful assistant disappear." He glanced at me and winked.

Once again, Norbert unfolded the paper sack and held it out to the audience. "See, nothing in the bag. Abbracadabra." He waved his

34

hand over the bag. Then he popped the bag over his head. "Ta da," he said. "Abbie has disappeared. But where did everyone else go? Oh no. I've made everyone disappear."

The audience laughed.

"I hear you, but I can't see you," Norbert said. "Everything's gone. I've made the whole room disappear. Abbracadabra." He pulled the sack off his head. "Hey, you're all back. Ladies and gentlemen, boys and girls, please give a big hand to my assistant, the beautiful Abbie."

The audience broke into applause.

Norbert the clown took my hand, squeezed it, and we both bowed.

"You were wonderful," Chrissy told me after the show. "Thank you so much for joining us here today."

"It was truly my pleasure," I told her.

As we walked out of the hospital, I felt a little bit sad to be leaving.

On the way home from the hospital, Wilson said, "Abbie, you were the best assistant ever. I hope you had fun."

"Thanks, Wilson. I had a great time. It was one of the best Thanksgivings I've ever had." I had so much fun that I felt guilty when I remembered how upset I'd been at not being able to go home for Thanksgiving.

As he drove, I glanced over at Wilson. It had been fun spending the day with him, almost like a date. Was he dating anyone? Would I ever see him again?

Say something, anything, I commanded myself. Ask if we can see each other again. Offer to give him your number. But no words came out of my mouth, until I said goodbye to Wilson at my door.

The man was a Prince Charming, even if he had been dressed like a clown. The clown prince probably had a girlfriend, maybe more than one.

Mom called not long after I got home. "How did it go?" she asked.

"It was really fun, Mom, and I probably wouldn't have done it if you hadn't suggested I volunteer." I told her all about my day with Wilson.

"He sounds like a special man," Mom said.

"He is, Mom, and I'm afraid I'll never see him again."

She laughed. "Isn't a little too early to give up on a man you just met?"

Of course, she was right. I didn't really know Wilson. All I could say was that I had spent the day with a man in a clown suit, a man whose face I'd never seen. But several times during the day, I had felt like I had caught a glimpse into Wilson's heart, and it was a beautiful place.

The next morning at the office, Shirley wanted to hear all about my day at the children's hospital. When I described the magic act, she laughed.

"I wish I could have been there," she said. "How did you like Wilson?"

"He's a nice guy," I said slowly. "Is he. . ."

"Dating anyone?" Shirley finished for me. "I don't think so."

"How do you know him?"

"He's my husband's best friend. They've known each other all their lives. Wilson spent a lot of time in the hospital when he was young. I think that's why he became a doctor. My husband, Bill, was one of the only kids who went to the hospital to visit Wilson. They used to practice magic together."

"Is Bill as good at magic as Wilson?" I asked.

"I don't think anyone is as good as Wilson, except for a few professional magicians. Wilson can do all kinds of tricks and illusions. But his favorite thing is to dress up like Norbert the clown and entertain the children. His last girlfriend wasn't too happy about that."

"She didn't like him entertaining the kids?"

"Nope. Judy said that by acting like a clown, Wilson was making a fool of himself, and by extension, he was making a fool of her. She wanted him to give it up. He wouldn't do it. So they broke up."

"Maybe she was trying to control him," I commented.

Shirley smiled. "That's exactly what she was trying to do. The first time I met Judy, I knew she wanted to get her hooks into Wilson. She had decided to marry him, but it didn't work out for her."

"What happened to her?"

My assistant shrugged. "I heard she moved to Kansas City. Her sister lives there, I think."

I was dying to ask her if she thought Wilson would be interested in going out with me, but I didn't know how to get the words out.

"Um, do you think. . ."

"Wilson might be interested in going out with you?" Shirley finished. "I wouldn't be surprised."

She was right, because later that afternoon, Wilson called me at work.

"Abbie, I'm sorry to bother you when you're working, but I just found out that I've got tomorrow night off and I was wondering if you would like to go and see a movie with me."

"I would love to," I told him. After I hung up, I walked over to Shirley's desk and said, "I've just made a date with a man I've never

36

seen. What does Wilson look like?"

She grinned. "So he did call you. I had a feeling he might. I'm not going to tell you what he looks like. Let's just say you won't be disappointed."

When Wilson arrived at my apartment the next evening, I discovered that he looked pretty much like I had expected. He had dark, curly hair and a straight nose, and he greeted me with a lopsided grin.

"I was wondering if you would recognize plain Wilson Mitchell," he said. "I know I'm not as handsome as Norbert the clown." His smile lit up his face and reminded me that he was a man who would always be able to see the humor in life.

"No one is as handsome as Norbert the clown. But I'm looking forward to getting to know plain Wilson Mitchell. There's just one thing I was wondering. Are you going to steal my watch again?"

"No, I'm not, Abbie. But you never know about a magician, he might steal your heart."

"You can do that with magic?" I asked.

"Love is the only real magic," Wilson said, "and there's love all around."

And when he kissed me goodnight after our first date, I felt the magic between us.

It's funny how things work out. Before Thanksgiving, I was thinking I would never meet anyone, never have any friends or dates in Mayfield. Now I have both. All I had to do was take a step outside of my own little world.

We're still entertaining the children on Thanksgiving, but now we bring our own kids along with us too. The clown prince turned out to be the man of my dreams.

THE END

THANKSGIVING IS A TIME
FOR REMEMBERING

It was the day before Thanksgiving. I was in my backyard, all alone. I thought about the last Thanksgiving, when Ben was still alive. I'd spent Thanksgiving at the nursing home. I missed him so very much. I missed our children, Chip and Mia, too.

Chip was living in Germany. He and his wife were in the Navy and stationed there. Mia was somewhere in Africa. My daughter worked for the big magazines. She was a wonderful photographer. She shot many spreads for well-known magazines and was out and about, seeing the world through her camera's eye—and making very good money doing so. If only Ben were still alive. I was so lonely without him.

When I trimmed the branches of the big oak tree in our yard, a nest fell out.

I picked it up and looked at it for a long time. I thought of how much time and work the mother bird had put into that little nest. How long Ben and I had worked getting our little cottage just so for the kids and for us . . . so many years of hard work.

How neat and perfect was each little twig that was placed in the little bird's nest. Just like me, that poor mother bird must have worked hard. I'd made every curtain for every window in my house with such care and perfection.

It is a perfect circle of love, I thought. So was my home with Ben and our two children growing up. I remembered Ben putting the little gym set out in the yard for them and how they loved to play on it out there. Mia would play on the swings for hours and hours, and Chip loved to play on the slide all day.

I thought about the bird that had made her nest. She sat there on her eggs through the storms, the rain, and the sunshine. I remembered all of the colds, measles, and bouts of chicken pox I'd gone through with my two and that Ben and I worried about them so much when they were ill.

The little bird was not much different than I was with my children. She never once thought of abandoning her nest or leaving it, except maybe to gather some food. I had grabbed many a "quick" bite so I could be with Mia at her dance recitals or at Chip's Little League games.

When the mother bird's little chicks were hatched, she carried food back to the nest and fed them. Ben worked so hard to provide for us.

As I looked at the little bird's nest, I thought about how she covered them with her wings and kept them safe in that circle of love. We were such a lucky, close-knit family, and my children were both so thankful to Ben and I for what they had. They both loved us very much, as much as we loved them. Our children were wonderful and I missed them.

But like the little bird, when the time came, she pushed them from the nest to fly on their own. I hated to see my two children grow up and leave their nest. I cried my eyes out the day Chip joined the military. I was happy for my daughter when she got her dream job of doing her creative craft, traveling and getting paid for it. I hated to see her go, but I just wanted her to be happy.

While under her wing and in her nest, the little bird must have felt like me. She'd been pleased that her children were safe and she never wanted to let them go, but now it was up to them to fly away and live their own lives. She had nurtured her babies as much as she could. But all babies grow up. I started to cry in my yard and grabbed for a tissue. If only Ben were still alive to be here with me. I thought a bit more out on that chilly day before Thanksgiving and thanked God for giving me such wonderful years with my husband and my two children.

What a lesson in motherhood I was getting from looking at that empty bird's nest.

And a reminder that I also had to let my children fly solo, as well.

But I thought about how after spending almost thirty years caring for my little birdies and to be alone in the nest now, I found myself going through a lot of changes.

I would now just fly around all day gathering food and come back home to an empty nest with no little mouths open for me to feed. The daddy bird was now gone, too.

I found myself chirping and no one chirped back anymore. The tears came down my cheeks as I thought about it some more. Then, I raked up the leaves Ben used to pile up high for the kids to jump into this time of year. I could just hear the echo of the children and my beloved husband laughing as they threw the autumn leaves at each other. On those days I would call them all into the house for one of my homemade pumpkin pies, and they'd gobble them down with hardy appetites.

Nowadays, I just didn't have an appetite, because like my little bird friend, it's no fun pecking around the feeder alone. Sometimes you get lonesome for the company of another bird, but probably like the little bird, there just didn't seem to be another one to replace her mate.

I know I didn't have it in my heart to replace Ben. We'd been happy and in love from the day we'd met when we were seventeen at a church social. When he asked me to dance, I thought I was in heaven in his arms and it was like that for every day of our lives together. I had been so very lucky.

So, like the little bird, you go back to your nest and sit there and wish for the old days, when your baby birdies were pecking around beside you and Daddy bird was right next to you. . . .

I went back into my house and cried my eyes out. I missed them all so much. The kids both called to wish me a Happy Thanksgiving, though. I lied to them both and told them I was going over to their Uncle Mark's house for dinner and that made them feel better. The truth was, I didn't plan to do anything on Thanksgiving Day.

I tried to sleep but just couldn't face the night in our lonely bed, so I lay down on the couch in the living room instead. I said a prayer to God to keep Ben safe in His arms and said a prayer to keep our children safe and sound, too. Then I just lay there and prayed to God for my soul for Him to keep, and I just couldn't stop crying and cried myself to sleep. I dozed off thinking about my husband.

I felt so badly thinking about the previous Thanksgiving at the nursing home with Ben. He was suffering so very much. The doctor had him on morphine, so he had been in and out of consciousness all that day. Ben had been a contractor and worked very hard. He was in the middle of building us a beautiful log cabin on the lake for our retirement. It was going to have a little dock for him so he could keep his sailboat there, and he also showed me plans for a wonderful loft on the top floor for me to have a little office, where I could do my writing.

It was my dream to one day write a children's book that would be published that I could read to my grandchildren. Ben didn't get to build our dream retirement home. He had lung cancer, and the doctors had done everything they could for him, but he was terminal and they put him in a nursing home nearby because beds were scarce at the hospital.

That Thanksgiving Day at the nursing home, Ben slept most of the time. He was really out of it. Our two children both phoned him from where they were to tell him that they loved and missed him, but they never got to talk to him. I'd gone down to the lobby for a while, and that's when I'd met Margie Seaver.

She was a lovely older woman in her nineties. I felt so sorry for her as I watched her. She was all dressed up in a lovely floral dress, with a pretty little hat and white gloves and shoes. She had a pair of pearl earrings on and a cameo on her dress that looked very old. She just sat there watching all the other patients who could leave for the day to have dinner with their families.

40

I asked her, "Are you waiting for someone to pick you up and take you to dinner?"

She answered, "Oh, yes! My husband, Bradford, will be here any minute to come and get me. He's just running late." That's when she told me her name was Margie Seaver and that she lived across the hall from my husband, Ben. She smiled at me.

That was when I heard another voice say, "Yes, Margie lives in Room 3, your Ben lives in 5, and my wife, Mallory, lives in Room 7." He held his hand out to me and said, "Hi, I'm Justin Khiel. How's your husband doing today? I've seen you around in the hallway."

I shook his hand. "Hi, I'm Lucy Sweetin. Ben isn't doing too well today, but thank-you," I said as Justin sat down on the bench in the lobby with Margie and me.

That day, Justin and I talked a lot. He told me all about how his poor wife and he had been driving one day to the grocery store, and how she just folded over on him in the car. He had to pull over and use his cell phone to call an ambulance. His wife had suffered an aneurysm and a loss of oxygen and was now brain-dead and on a respirator. Justin had told me that his wife was only in her early fifties. I could relate to him because Ben was, too. It was such a shame that both their lives were being cut so short.

As we talked, Margie told us that she loved roses and that she missed pruning her roses in her yard. She told us that her husband was taking fine care of them, though.

That's when the nurse came over and said, "Margie, it's time to come for Thanksgiving dinner. You've been sitting here since nine this morning, and it's noon, now. Come on and get something to eat." The nurse looked at her.

"No, I'm expecting company. My husband is just running late. He will be here to take me home and see my roses in my garden and eat Thanksgiving dinner with him." The old woman smiled and was happy with her thoughts. The nurse just started to walk away. Then she told us, "Her husband has been dead for years. Margie's suffering from Alzheimer's disease."

Justin and I looked at one another sadly, then at Margie. We tried to take her with us to the cafeteria in the home, but she wouldn't come. We talked some more about our mates and how much they were suffering, and I hardly touched my food. He told me how his wife had loved her rosebushes so much, too—just like poor Margie. Justin talked about how he missed her loving little touches around the house now that she was no longer there.

He talked about his children, too, who were all grown up and had families of their own. He told me how much his wife had loved her grandchildren. It was all such a tragedy for us it seemed, that day.

Justin went back to his wife's room and I went back to Ben's, and I didn't see Justin again after Ben had died. Ben died just before Christmas last year, and it was horrible and lonely for me.

That Thanksgiving morning when I woke, I had a stiff neck from lying on the couch. The sun blinded me, streaming in through the window as it woke me up from a dream about Ben. I stumbled over to the coffeepot and made myself some coffee when I realized that it was Thanksgiving.

I thought about the little bird in her nest, and how she always took care of her own. I wanted to do something nice for someone— even if it wasn't one of my own. I got this idea of poor Margie and thought it might be nice if I went over to the nursing home and brought her a few roses and see how she was doing. I drove out there and I ran into Justin in the lobby.

"Hi, there, Lucy—how's Ben?" he asked. "I haven't been around much anymore," he said.

"How's Mallory?" I asked him almost in unison.

Seemingly together, we answered: "Ben's passed—"

"Mallory's gone—"

We just looked at each other, in surprise, as I asked, "Who're you visiting here, then?"

"I came here to say hello to Margie."

I looked at him and said, "Me, too. I was feeling sorry for myself, and lonely."

Justin looked at me and said, "Lucy, so was I."

The nurse came over and we asked how Margie was doing and she told us that Margie was gone, too. I looked at Justin; we'd both had flowers in our hands to give to her. We stood there in dismay, and finally Justin said to me, "Lucy, would you like to come over to my house for some turkey? It isn't a real turkey. I only have two frozen turkey dinners in my freezer, but you're welcome to come, if you'd like. I don't like spending Thanksgiving alone, either." He looked at me with such sad, lonely eyes, and I could tell that he felt as badly as I did.

"Sure, why not?" We drove off to his home in the snow. I didn't know where he lived but I found myself driving with him out to the lake.

When we got there, I couldn't believe my eyes; he lived in a beautiful log home on the lake, just like Ben was trying to build for me.

It was lovely as we ate our dinner and talked all night while the snow fell. We spoke about our lost spouses, and how much we loved them and how wonderful our lives had been together. We talked about our children and his grandchildren and our dreams for the future and also how lonely we both were.

It took us a year and a half of seeing one another and leaning on one another, but, somehow, we fell in love. The grief over our spouses became joy in our hearts, knowing that they both wanted to see us happy here on earth. It was hard at first seeing that my life could go on and would go on without Ben and that I didn't have to be alone like my little bird friend in her nest. So I decided I could fly away with Justin into a new nest.

I moved into Justin's nest, the log home on the lake that Ben and I had always wanted. I know he is smiling down on me from up above. I also thank my friend, Margie Seaver, for bringing Justin and me together.

I felt so sorry for that poor old woman, all dressed up with nowhere to go on Thanksgiving. Now, when I look at Mallory's rosebushes in front of the house, I think about all three that are gone from us. I think about Margie being with her beloved husband in heaven, and about my beloved Ben, and also Mallory. I know they are all happy up there together and smiling down on Justin and me.

Justin and I are married now, and I'm writing my children's book in the loft of my log cabin on the lake for my grandchildren to read. My daughter, Mia, married and has a baby girl, and my son, Chip and his wife now have two boys. I see my children all the time now, and I have Justin's children and their children to love, also. Now there are a lot of baby chicks in our nest to love!

THE END

IT'S MY FIRST THANKSGIVING
I Can't Look Like A Turkey Today!

"Just put your fingers around the edge of the pie like this and give the dough a gentle twist," Barbara said, as her fingers expertly left a row of perfect scallops around the pie.

Following my sister-in-law's example, I put my fingers on the edge of the pie dough and gave a gentle twist. My fingernail immediately pierced the dough, creating a hole.

"We can mend that with a little water," Barbara said quickly, reaching for the glass of chilled water we'd used earlier to mend the crusts I'd rolled out. "Try again," she urged, slowly making a scallop so I could see how it was done.

I didn't want to try again! But I had to, if I was ever going to master pie making before Thanksgiving dinner, which was only a few days away. My touch was gentler this time and although my scallops weren't as perfect as Barbara's, I didn't break through the dough. I carefully continued around the pie until I was done.

"You did it!" Barbara said, standing back and admiring my work.

"But it isn't perfect," I said softly. Even a non-critical eye could easily see that my scallops were too thin in some places and too thick in others.

"This isn't my first pie," she said with a smile. "Let's put them in the oven so they're done by dinner." With experienced ease, Barbara adjusted the oven racks, slid the apple pies into the oven, and set the timer.

She was the best sister-in-law in the world and was so patient with me. I don't know what I would've done if she hadn't offered to give me a quick course in pie baking. I knew what I'd like to do—go to the bakery and buy pies. But in Mike's family, pies from a bakery would never do. Mike's mother and sister were expert cooks and never bought anything from bakeries or in-store deli departments.

It wasn't that I couldn't cook. I made spaghetti, broiled tasty steaks, and fixed a pretty good meat loaf. But pies, turkeys, stuffing, and homemade rolls were way out of my league. I'd never prepared a holiday dinner—until now.

Only three days until The Day, I thought solemnly. Mike's looking forward to Thanksgiving as much as I'm dreading it.

We decided to host the family Thanksgiving dinner a couple of months ago when we moved from our duplex into our house. The day we moved in, Mike stood in the dining room with his arm wrapped around my shoulders and said, "Now that we have a big dining room we can have family dinners." To Mike, a family dinner meant including all his aunts, uncles, grandparents, and anyone else somehow related. We hadn't been able to have family dinners before because our duplex was too small.

"The table we bought will be large enough for everyone in the family," I said, imaging his family sitting around the table set with my new white linen cloth and my best china.

"The next big holiday is Thanksgiving; let's invite everyone for dinner," he suggested, his eyes dancing at the idea.

His enthusiasm was contagious and I immediately agreed. I wanted to entertain his family and build on the good relationships I had with them. Most of all, I wanted Mike to be proud of me as a wife who prepared a holiday meal for his family. As the months passed and the holiday neared, my enthusiasm faded as I realized what I'd volunteered to do.

Barbara's voice interrupted my thoughts. "Here's the recipe for Grandma's turkey stuffing," she said, handing me a recipe card.

"Thanks," I said, groaning inwardly as my eyes quickly surveyed the long list of ingredients—many which were unfamiliar to me.

"Let me know if there's anything I can do to help."

"I think you've done enough already by giving me the pie-making lessons, and now the family stuffing recipe," I said with a smile. I'd love her help, but I didn't want Mike or his family to think I wasn't capable of preparing a Thanksgiving dinner.

"Smells good in here," Mike said as he came into the kitchen with Rick, his brother-in-law, following close behind. They'd been watching a football game on television in the family room.

"It's the stew," Rick said, walking over to the crock-pot and peeking through the lid.

"From the hungry looks on your faces, the football game must be over," Barbara joked.

"Playing couch football really builds up an appetite," Mike joked back, with a smile.

"We just need to set the table and then we can eat," Barbara said, opening the refrigerator and lifting out a bowl with tossed salad.

"I'll get the silverware and bowls," I said, thankful that there was one task I could do without personal instructions or a recipe.

As we sat around the table laughing and talking, I thought how lucky I was to have married into a family who so easily accepted me. Being loved and accepted weren't things I took for granted. I always felt that my dad didn't like me. When I was in kindergarten he moved out of the house and I never saw him again. While I'm sure he left because of relationship problems with my mother, I always felt that he didn't like me since he never attempted to see me after he left.

I'd spent most of my life trying to achieve love and acceptance from my mother without success. Mom had a natural gift of gab and made friends with everyone she met. She was an alcoholic; the more she drank, the more outgoing she became. I was shy and not overly talkative—totally the opposite of Mom. She was always critical of my quietness and often tried to draw me out by asking me embarrassing questions in front of her friends, especially after she'd had several drinks. Her questions left me tongue-tied and my responses usually brought snickers and odd looks from her friends. Memories of those times were scarred on my heart forever.

Although she helped me with my college expenses, she always criticized my decision to be a high school science teacher. She'd shake her head and say, "That's a man's job," or, "With a job like that you'll wind up a spinster."

Unfortunately, she died of liver disease from her drinking before she saw me graduate from college and marry Mike. He and his family were so loving and welcoming to me that I cherished every moment with them. I wanted to do everything I could to continue to be accepted and belong—that's why Thanksgiving dinner was so important to me.

The next afternoon it was the end of the school day and I was cleaning up from a science experiment when my friend, Lily, walked in. Lily was not only a friend, but she was a great source of cooking information since she was the home economics teacher.

"Here's my recipe for butterflake rolls," she said, handing me a sheet of paper.

"I owe you a lunch for all the help you've given me," I said with a smile. Last week Lily gave me her no-fail recipes for roasting turkey, making gravy, and pumpkin pie filling.

She waved her hand, dismissing the lunch, "I'm just glad to help you."

"I wish holiday dinners were as easy as science experiments," I said as I slipped a test tube in the rack.

"Don't let this dinner wear you down," she said. "Remember to enjoy yourself."

"Sure," I said with a laugh. Leave it to Lily to make a joke.

"I'm not kidding, Jodi. Don't get yourself in such a sweat over this dinner that you don't enjoy your family. That's what the holidays are about—appreciating your loved ones, and enjoying yourself."

Enjoying myself was the furthest thing from my mind. All I wanted to do was prepare a dinner Mike would be proud of, and not embarrass myself in front of his family.

I had the day before Thanksgiving off, so I planned to spend

46

the day baking pies, preparing stuffing ingredients, and making homemade rolls. Mike had to work, so I had the house to myself. As the day progressed, I was glad he wasn't home to watch my kitchen disasters and mishaps. He was due home in about an hour when I was finished with my tasks, or as finished as I was going to be. The kitchen was filled with dirty pans, open sacks of flour and sugar, and a pile of food-spotted recipe cards. On the kitchen table, carefully concealed under dishtowels, were the results of my day in the kitchen.

I leaned against the counter and sighed as I stared at the table. I didn't need to look under the dishtowels to see what was there—the images were all too vivid. My pumpkin pies would probably taste good, but they certainly didn't have an experienced baker's appearance. I'd forgotten how Barbara made her scallops on the crust, so I improvised. My edges weren't even or symmetrical, and now were thick and bulky after they were baked.

My butterflake rolls were small and heavy, not light and airy like Mike's mom's rolls. The bread for the stuffing was cubed, but I was afraid my cubes were too big. If I cut them in half they would be too small. I didn't have any more bread, so I'd have to make do with the cubes I had. My review of the day was interrupted as Mike came in the door.

"I got off early," he said, giving me a quick kiss on the lips. I was happy that he'd gotten off early for the holiday, but was disappointed the kitchen was still in chaos.

"I have a bit of cleaning-up to do," I said, moving toward the pile of pans waiting by the sink.

"What do we have here?" he asked, walking toward the kitchen table.

"No peeking," I said in a teasing tone as I slipped between him and the table. I couldn't bear for him to see my baking disasters until tomorrow. I kept thinking maybe they would look better when they were on the table with the other food; or perhaps with the excitement of company, he may not notice how things looked or tasted. Not realistic thinking, but it was the only hope I had.

"How about some help washing the dishes, then?" he said, nodding toward the stack of pans and sticky bowls.

"Sure," I said, moving toward him and slipping my arms around his neck and giving him a grateful hug.

"And, how about calling out for a pizza tonight?" he said, giving me a kiss on the nose.

"Hawaiian on my half," I joked, thinking how wonderful he was to help with dishes and dinner.

While we washed the dishes, I kept glancing at the table and picturing my baking efforts. I was forcing myself to be in a light mood, but in my heart I was dreading the next day. I was going to be embarrassed for myself and for Mike. He was counting so much on this dinner, and I knew he was picturing a meal at his mother's or Barbara's, not something put together by an amateur. I remembered Lily's comment about enjoying the day and sighed. I was not enjoying myself, and tomorrow would be no better.

The next morning I let Mike sleep in while I worked on the dinner. The first thing I did was look at my pies, hoping they appeared better than I remembered, but they looked even less professional than they had yesterday. A squeeze test of the rolls told me they had gotten harder overnight. As I mixed the stuffing, it looked too chunky, but maybe it would blend together better after it baked.

After setting the table, I stepped back and looked at the room. I was proud of the table—with my new white linen cloth, good china, and a floral arrangement of golden and red mums.

"We're going to have a wonderful dinner," Mike said, coming up behind me, and wrapping his arms around me.

He was still in his pajamas when he hugged me. How would he feel after our dinner? In my heart I knew I was going to make a fool of myself and disappoint him.

By the time Mike's family began arriving, I'd showered and changed into an emerald green sleeveless dress. After greeting our guests, I left Mike in the living room serving champagne and sparkling cider, and went back to the kitchen.

"Need any help?" Barbara and her mother said, sticking their heads into the kitchen.

"No, thanks," I said, forcing my voice to sound happy and under control.

"It's so nice of you to have us for Thanksgiving," his mother said, giving me a kiss on the cheek.

I ushered them back to the living room and then began to tackle mashing the potatoes and making the gravy. Mike would carve the turkey at the table. Judging from the turkey's golden brown skin and wonderful fragrance it would be a success.

Even though I followed Lily's no-fail recipe, the gravy was lumpy. Stirring and smashing the lumps didn't help. I let it simmer while I reluctantly put my rolls in the breadbasket, and cut my pies. They looked worse than I remembered. As for the rolls, they'd make good golf balls. I looked at the pan with the gravy of lumps, the chunky stuffing, and my baking attempts. Tears filled my eyes.

"I'm back to offer last-minute help," Barbara said as she walked into the kitchen. I didn't want her to see my tears, so I turned toward the range and busied myself with the gravy while I bit my lip. But the emotional pain was too great and I couldn't stop the tears.

She came up beside me, not aware of my tears, until she looked at my face.

"Jodi, you're crying," she said softly, putting her hand on my shoulder that was beginning to shake as my crying became more intense. "What's wrong?"

"My dinner."

She kept her arm on my shoulder and looked around the kitchen. "It looks all done."

"It's a mess," I said, finally turning to face her. "My pies look like I used my elbows to make the crust, the rolls are like rocks, my stuffing is too chunky, and now my gravy has lumps."

"Oh, honey," she said, pulling me into her arms.

"I've ruined Mike's day," I said through my tears.

"Who's ruined my day?" Mike said in a joking tone.

Just what I need, I thought at the sound of his voice. Oh well, he may as well find out now what a disaster the dinner is.

"We're just handling a few last minute details," Barbara said, handing me a paper towel to wipe my eyes.

"She's being kind," I said.

"The turkey looks great," Mike said, obviously trying to make me feel better.

"The turkey probably turned out all right," I agreed, "but the rest of the dinner isn't up to the quality that your family is used to. I wanted everything to be perfect."

"Everything is perfect," Mike said. "We're all together as a family. That's what matters."

He's echoing Lily's words, I thought. But it's easy for him to feel that way because he didn't prepare a disastrous dinner.

"I don't have the knack at cooking like Barbara and your mother," I whispered.

"Maybe cooking isn't your forte, but that doesn't mean we love you any less or that the holiday is ruined," Barbara said, giving my arm a comforting squeeze. "Thanksgiving isn't about smooth gravy and perfect pie crust. It's about being with family, and enjoying being together."

"Honey, I love you and your dinner is going to be just fine," Mike said, pulling me into his arms and holding me tight. He laid his head on top of mine and rubbed my back until my tears stopped. Reluctantly I left his warm embrace and stood looking at the kitchen, filled with the food to be served.

Barbara wrapped her arm around my shoulder, steering me toward the bedroom. "Jodi, go fix your makeup while my brother and I manage the kitchen for a few minutes."

When I returned with fresh eye shadow and mascara I discovered the gravy had lost its lumps, the crust edges had been removed and replaced with a decorative trim of whipping cream, and the rolls, while not perfect, were softer.

"Let's get the food on the table," Barbara said, handing me the turkey to carry to the table.

Minutes later I sat at the dining room table, surrounded by people filled with love and appreciation for each other. I'd learned the true meaning of Thanksgiving, and how the holiday is about enjoying and being thankful for our families. A perfect Thanksgiving isn't about the dinner; it is about being with people you love and who love you. When Mike reached over and gave me a hug, and Barbara winked at me, I knew that this was a perfect Thanksgiving Day.

THE END

TGI . . . THANKSGIVING!
How Turkey Day worked its magic on me

You will be killed or seriously injured if you don't follow instructions!

I slowly placed the instruction manual down and backed away from the counter. Because my eyes were locked on the food processor in front of me, I nearly fell over the carton it came in.

I saw red—and the cheery woman on the box gushing, Makes cooking and baking a breeze!

I aimed for her nose and kicked. The box bounced, and the packaging materials flew everywhere. I left them where they lay, as a warning to myself for the next time a culinary brainstorm struck.

If I knew I'd end up being the owner of the chainsaw of kitchen appliances, I never would have undertaken this project. I have trouble enough preparing a recipe with the usual equipment. All that chopping, dicing, and slicing make me blanch. Making modeling dough cupcakes, like the preschool kids I teach showed me, is more my speed: no tools required.

But I'd decided to give the kitchen arts another try because, just this once, my mother may have been right. "The way to a man's heart is through his stomach," she told me. And told me. And told me.

I was due for an "I told you so." My significant other became insignificant recently. Just my luck—he left me for a line cook. Unless I found a replacement for him before Mom's big Thanksgiving dinner, I'd be eating crow while everyone else ate turkey.

Thanks to my miscalculation regarding the power tool disguised as a kitchen helper, I needed a new strategy. No way was I risking life and limb for a tofu pumpkin pie.

That meant the vegan singles' potluck supper was out.

The potluck was my best friend, Bridget's, idea, anyway. I didn't even know what "vegan" was until she explained it to me. Of course, at ten days from the holiday and counting, guys who are "vegetarian to the max" didn't sound so bad. At eight days, minus a plan, they sounded out of reach.

The phone rang. It was Bridget.

"Hey, Amaya," she said. "Have fun tonight. Keep your eyes peeled for Joaquin."

By "Joaquin" she meant Joaquin Phoenix, my latest Hollywood crush. Bridget swore to me he's a vegan. Knowing she'd say anything to get me to the singles' event, I had my doubts. She felt guilty for introducing me to my ex; it showed in her determination to get me matched again.

"I'm not going," I said.

"Why not? Don't you feel well?"

"Not especially." I told her why.

"So, go without it."

"What?"

"The pie. Say you forgot it. The food's not important."

"But Larry—"

"Larry left you for a piece of rump, girlfriend. And I don't mean rump roast. Your cooking had nothing to do with it."

"Mom says—" I started to say, but she cut me off again.

"Your mom says a lot of things. Trust me, people don't go to singles' meetings to eat. Get your own rump in gear, and get going."

I laughed. I had my orders. Besides, I liked her reasoning. "I'll call you tomorrow."

Thinking to make up in eye candy for what I lacked in solid fare, I dressed for the supper in my shortest skirt. I checked my look in the mirror. Not bad. Larry, a meat-and-potatoes man, liked my legs; maybe a vegan guy would, too. Granted, the mini wasn't the best choice for a frigid November evening. So I'd catch a cold. Who cares? It's better than not catching a man.

"Let's get this party started," I said to my reflection. I pulled on my coat and left for the health food store annex, where the vegan singles meet.

The instant I drove up to the building, I knew my luck hadn't changed one iota. The annex was dark. The parking lot was empty. At twenty-three past the hour, the supper should've been in full swing. I slumped in my seat. This wasn't my day.

I was about to turn the car around and head for home when, out of the corner of my eye, I noticed movement. I squinted through the side window for a better look. Then I saw it: a note attached to the annex door. Its unsecured end was flapping in the wind.

My mood took another turn. All is not lost yet! Maybe the meeting is rescheduled for tomorrow. I parked in one of the empty slots and hurried over with my fingers crossed to read what the note said.

Vegan singles' potluck supper cancelled.

Before I got the chance to be disappointed, a voice behind me asked, "Are you here for the potluck, too?"

I spun around. Joaquin Phoenix didn't sneak up behind me, but this guy's smile was just as nice as my Hollywood heartthrob's.

"Where'd you come from?" I gasped. My heart was racing from the fright.

"I live over there," the dark-haired guy with the sexy dimple said. He nodded toward a small house across the road. "Sorry. I didn't mean to scare you. I was hoping someone besides me would show up. I made enough food for an army."

A man who cooks—how cool is that! He was good at it, too, from what I could tell of the body under his bulky jacket. It takes more than rabbit food to grow shoulders like those.

My heart was still racing, but the reason changed. My mind went from the kitchen to the bedroom in sixty seconds. I pushed away the thought before I drooled all over my carefully chosen outfit.

"What did you make?" I asked.

"Ribs."

Ribs? Bridget said vegans consume no—as in none whatsoever—animal products. Is this guy an imposter like me? "You eat meat?"

"Vital wheat gluten."

"Excuse me?"

"I molded them out of vital wheat gluten."

Ahh—the old vital wheat gluten trick. Not only was he attractive and friendly, he was also resourceful. I wondered if he was handy with a food processor.

"Sounds. . . ." I groped for a word. "Interesting. I have tofu pumpkin pie back at my place. I . . . umm . . . forgot to bring it."

"No kidding! Pumpkin pie's my favorite. When I went vegan, it was the one thing I couldn't give up. I miss my mother's."

"Oh. I'm sorry."

He laughed. "That didn't come out right. Mom's alive and well. But since she and my dad retired to New Mexico, I don't get home for the holidays much. Airfare's outrageous. At least on my salary."

"Too bad," I said, thinking, Too good to be true! I pictured him at my family's dining room table. "What kind of work do you do?"

"I'm a conservation officer at the preserve."

Conservation officer. That has a meat-and-potatoes ring to it. "Is that anything like a cop?"

"We're required to have law enforcement officer certification."

"So, you are a cop? I mean, like, you carry a gun and everything?"

"My job is to protect wildlife. A firearm's one of my tools. Why? Are you afraid of guns?" He cocked his head in a way Larry never did—as if he really wanted to know.

"A little," I said. "Mostly, I'm afraid of knives."

"I'd say you have a healthy respect for objects with a potential for serious bodily injury."

That settled it; it was time to act. I was picking up good vibes from my fellow single. But any moment, someone with a skirt shorter than mine could turn up, and I'd have to share him. Or, possibly, lose him. I couldn't let this one get away. Not to mention I was turning into a Popsicle in my own short skirt.

"Well put." I stuck out my hand for him to shake. "I'm Amaya."

"Amaya. That's different."

My spirits fell. Another critic—just like Mom and Larry.

My feelings must've shown on my face because he quickly added, "Different is good. My name's Warren."

He took my hand. Given the temperature, his touch was surprisingly warm. I was glad I forgot my mittens. My stomach did a backflip. It didn't take much to revive my spirits.

"Nice night," I said to get the conversation back on track.

"Yes, it is."

"Except for. . . ."

"What?"

"You know." I faked a shiver. "The cold."

"I'm outside all day. I'm used to it. But you. . . ." His dark eyes flickered over me, and I felt a different kind of warmth. "You must be freezing. And here I am, keeping you. What am I thinking?"

I smiled. "I know what I'm thinking."

"What's that?"

"Oh, just that I'm ravenous."

"Ravenous." He nodded. "That's a definite."

"So, if I'm ravenous. . . ."

"Yes?"

"And you're ravenous. . . ."

"Yes?"

"What do you think about grabbing those ribs and following me back to my apartment?" Although I kept the smile on my face, my insides were churning. I'd be so ready to die if he refused.

Instead, he grinned. "I guess you didn't get my hint about the pumpkin pie."

I laughed with relief and something more—surprise. Maybe there was some truth to that heart-stomach thing. "You're very subtle."

"I'll have to work on my technique. Come on, I'll walk you to your car. Unless you'd rather come with me to the house and meet my dog."

"I don't know. . . ." Dogs also have potential for serious bodily injury. "Is it a big dog?"

"Rebel's a shepherd."

"I think I'll wait in the car."

"He likes people."

"Maybe another time."

"Okay. I wouldn't want you to do anything you're uncomfortable with."

He touched his hand to the small of my back, and we started for the lot. The brief physical contact gave me a nice feeling. It was gentle, yet protective. Controlled force is probably one of those concepts a conservation officer has to master. I imagined Warren knew how to hold his own with any threat.

Once I was safe inside my car with the heater blasting, he said, "Lock your doors. I'll try not to be long. Rebel can have his nature break while I get the stuff together."

"Take whatever time you need," I said. "I'll be all right."

He looked as good from the back as he did from the front. I watched him walk off with long, confident strides and smiled. He's the male animal at its finest. The best part is, I met him a whole eight days before Thanksgiving.

As soon as the thought crossed my mind, I wished it didn't. It awakened the part of my head where my mother resides. I imagined her scolding that I topped even myself this time. I didn't know Warren from Adam—yet I was bringing him home with me. Instincts aren't to be trusted; cold, hard facts are. I'm more likely to be murdered by a stranger than to be diced to death by a food processor. If I didn't get out of there, I'm too stupid to live—and probably wouldn't.

I looked toward the small house across the road. I'm starting to change my mind, Warren. Please hurry!

My silent plea went unanswered. The occupant of the house was nowhere in sight, and the voice of doom grew louder. As usual, I was damned if I did, damned if I didn't.

Finally, I gave in to the voice and fled, feeling like I wanted to barf.

I never would have made it as a getaway driver. I must have hit every red light between the annex and home. Then there was the lost out-of-towner I got stuck behind. And the cat that darted into my path. (By some miracle, it wasn't black). I missed it by a hair.

Just outside the town center, I picked up a tailgater. After a block of hugging my bumper, the driver flashed me with his high beams. He was driving a pickup, so the whole interior of my car lit with the glare. I didn't need an aggressive driver riding my butt, too. I slowed and edged closer to the curb to let him pass.

Be my guest, bozo, I thought. Doesn't this clown know a vehicle can be as deadly as any food processor?

Instead of passing, the pickup pulled in behind me. It was then that I realized what I should have a block ago. It's Warren! I stopped the car.

Warren emerged from the pickup. I held my breath as I watched him striding toward me. His masculine grace made me think lustful thoughts. The wind tousled his hair like I wanted to.

"Amaya." His deep voice sounded muffled through the glass.

Reluctantly, I cracked the window. "Oh, hi," I said, like the dork I am. "What are you doing here?"

"I'm practicing not being subtle. Where are you going?"

"I . . . umm . . . remembered I have something to do." Go home, pull the covers over my head, and pray this day from hell would end!

"What do you have to do that's so urgent?"

Good question. "It . . . umm . . . slipped my mind again."

"Can't be all that important. Are we still on for ribs and pie?"

Are we? Nothing changed, really—except now I was doubly charmed by him. He tracked me all this way!

Psycho killer, my mother's voice whispered.

"I don't think so," I said to Warren. I fiddled with the key chain dangling from the ignition to keep from looking at him.

"You're having second thoughts, aren't you?"

I looked at him then. He was smiling his nice, dimpled smile.

"Smart woman. Better to be safe than sorry." He pulled a cell phone from his pocket and began punching in numbers. "I have an idea."

"Who are you calling?"

"One of my references. She'll vouch for me."

"Warren—"

"Mom? It's me. Fine, fine. Listen, I have someone here who wants to talk with you. No, you don't know her—yet. I'll put her on."

He dropped the phone through the opening in the window. It fell in my lap. I gaped. "What? You want me to talk to your mother? What am I supposed to say? She'll think I'm crazy!"

He waved for me to pick it up. "Don't keep her hanging. She's a busy lady."

I must admit, I was curious. I put the phone to my ear. "Hello, Mrs.. . . ." I turned to Warren. I raised my eyebrows in question.

"Wilson," I thought he mouthed.

I covered the mouthpiece. "Did you say—"

"Mrs. Wilson. Mother of Mr. Wilson." He laughed at the joke he obviously told before.

I rolled my eyes. "Mrs. Wilson? Are you still there?"

"Who's this?" the woman on the phone asked.

"Amaya," I said. "I'm, uh, a friend of your son."

"Hello, Amaya. Can I help you with something?"

"No. Warren was just looking for an excuse to tell his Mr. Wilson joke." I glanced over at him. He was still grinning.

"He gets more like his father every day."

"Sorry to bother you."

"No bother. Tell him to bring you to New Mexico the next time he comes. I miss meeting his friends."

Warren missed her pumpkin pie. She missed meeting his friends. Clearly, what they really missed was each other. I thought of my relationship with my mother and felt my throat constrict. I had to get off the phone with Mrs. Wilson, or I'd start blubbering.

"Thank you," I said, hoping she couldn't hear the emotion in my voice. "I'm putting Warren back on. Nice chatting with you." I passed the phone back to him.

He talked another minute, then ended the call. "How about it?" he asked me.

"How about what?" I asked. My thoughts were still on Mrs. Wilson.

"The pie."

It occurred to me that the way to his heart really was through his stomach. I couldn't help but laugh. "You make it hard to say no," I said.

"That's the idea."

I turned the key in the ignition, he ran back to his truck, and the rest of the drive passed uneventfully.

Warren's acceptance managed to do what I alone couldn't: quiet the voice in my head.

The kitchen was in the same state I left it—chaos. I toed the appliance packaging aside, and we waded in.

"Well," I said. "Here we are."

Warren didn't appear to notice the mess. He went straight to the stove with his pan of vital wheat gluten ribs and opened the oven door.

"Do you mind?" he asked. "They have to be warmed up." He looked like he belonged there. I wanted him to belong there. A take-charge guy in my kitchen is my fantasy.

"Go right ahead," I said. "Let me take your jacket."

He set the temperature on the oven timer, which, by the way, I don't know how to operate, then handed me his coat. It smelled of the great outdoors—fresh and spicy.

"Now, let's see that pumpkin pie," he said.

I hugged his jacket to my chest. "I did mention it's tofu pumpkin pie, didn't I?"

"You did. It's amazing the things a person can do with tofu."

I was thinking more about the things a person couldn't do. "As long as we're straight on that. . . ." I gestured toward the counter. "There it is."

Warren looked at the aseptic brick of silken tofu. The canned pumpkin and bottle of maple syrup. The container of ground cloves I had to buy for the measly eighth of a teaspoon the recipe calls for. The cinnamon, the ginger. The salt—the only ingredient not newly purchased from the store. The pre-made vegan shell for the crust.

They were all spread across the counter, conspicuously separate. In the middle of it all, the food processor loomed.

"I don't see it," Warren said.

He still didn't get it.

"Look harder."

He looked again. Then he started to laugh. And laugh. "I was brought here under false pretenses," he said when he finally caught his breath.

"You insisted," I said. "You're not mad, are you?"

"Because a pretty woman lured me to her apartment? Hell, no! I'm flattered."

"I'm not sure 'lure' is the right word," I said, though it was. "Thanks for being okay with it."

"It seems like you were off to a good start. What happened?"

I draped his jacket over the back of a chair and picked up the food processor manual. I opened it to page one and showed him. "I was threatened with serious bodily injury."

He read the warning and began laughing again. "I never met anyone like you, Amaya. Show me the recipe."

I did eventually confess to being a meat eater. I couldn't pretend the vital wheat gluten ribs were good. But with Warren, I didn't have to.

The tofu pumpkin pie, on the other hand, was great—once he got around to making it.

The chef was even more complimentary. "Incredible," he said. He forked another bite into his mouth. "Mom will never believe how much this pie tastes like hers. You've got a killer recipe here."

"Made by a killer appliance," I said. "That's why I need someone armed and dangerous around."

"You got him, babe."

He leaned over and kissed me. And whetted my appetite for more.

"Ever been to New Mexico?" he asked.

"No, I haven't."

"What are you doing for Thanksgiving?"

THE END

A THANKFUL THANKSGIVING

I was so upset. "Alden, what are we going to do about Thanksgiving? Your parents expect us at their house, and my parents expect the same thing." I left the kitchenette, and I sat down next to my husband on the couch. "We can't be in two places at the same time."

"Um," was my husband's noncommittal reply from behind his newspaper.

"Pay attention," I scolded, snatching away his paper. "If we go to your parents' house, my parents will feel slighted, and vice versa."

Alden leaned over and tweaked my nose. "You worry too much, Suze," he said. "We'll have Thanksgiving dinner here for both our parents."

I froze. "Have them here?" I squeaked. "It would be a disaster."

"Why?"

"For one thing, we've never invited them to our apartment for dinner," I said, fishing for a reason to nix his suggestion.

"So, what difference does that make? Besides, it's about time we did. We've been married almost six months. I'll bet they'll jump at the chance to spend our first Thanksgiving with us."

"I've never cooked a turkey!" I was grasping at straws, desperate to avoid telling my husband the real reason for my reticence.

Alden cocked one quizzical eyebrow at me. "That's silly. You know how to cook."

"Meals, yes, but not a feast."

"You can do it, honey." My husband snaked his hand toward his newspaper.

"It wouldn't work." I visualized Alden's parents and my folks sitting with us and visibly shuddered.

Alden ignored his newspaper and reached for my hand instead. "This is about my mother and father, isn't it?"

"They hate me—especially your mother," I said as I wailed.

"My parents don't hate you." Alden kissed my fingers, but for once, I didn't melt at his touch. Just the thought of being in the presence of the Wellingtons, Alden's parents, for a lengthy meal, made my blood run cold.

"Yes, they do! Your mother was very vocal about how I wasn't good enough for you until the day of our marriage. Since then, on the rare occasions we're with her, she treats me like . . . like . . . a nonentity. Your father isn't very friendly, either."

59

"It's true you don't have a close relationship yet with Mother and Dad," Alden agreed, "but it'll come in time."

"Close relationship? We have no relationship whatsoever. Your parents have never welcomed me into their family like mine welcomed you into ours."

"Your parents are terrific!" Alden said and smiled. "I like them."

"Well, your parents are snobs," I snapped, "and I don't like them. So there!"

After a few additional cutting remarks on my part, I eventually agreed to host Thanksgiving dinner because I didn't have a choice. As I lay in bed after my husband went to sleep, I dreaded the upcoming event to the point where I felt physically sick.

As I busied myself in the kitchen early Thanksgiving morning, I contemplated what was to come. The Wellingtons were wealthy blue bloods who'd expected their son to marry someone from their economic strata. The fact that Alden and I were obviously madly in love didn't matter to them. They could focus only on their son's intended bride. I, Suze Browning, was not only just a lowly waitress, but also came from a blue-collar background. My father worked a county job, and my mother took in sewing on the side to augment Dad's low wages.

I vividly recalled Mrs. Wellington's horrified expression when Alden and I stated our intentions to become engaged.

"God forbid!" she exclaimed, staring at her son. "You plan to marry this . . . girl from across the railroad tracks? I forbid it. We forbid it."

Her cruel remark stated in my presence cut me to the quick, and it caused Alden to explode.

"I love Suze, and we intend to get married in June whether or not it meets with your approval! If you wish to attend our wedding, that's great. If you choose to stay home, it's your loss."

"Force our son to see what a mistake he's making!" Alden's mother addressed his father who was standing behind her.

"Your mother's right," Mr. Wellington said, reluctantly. "I'm sure Suze is a lovely girl, but she's not our kind. Think of your future. You want a wife who will be comfortable within our circle of friends."

Alden flounced out of their house, dragging me with him. "I'm sorry, my love, for putting you through that," he apologized. "Sometimes my parents can be very narrow-minded."

I was angry and hurt because my pride had taken an awful pounding. "Perhaps they're right," I told him. "I wouldn't fit in with their circle of friends."

"We'll make our own friends," Alden said, comforting me in his arms. "I can't live without you, Suze. Let's try and put this behind us."

60

Because I loved Alden so much, I attempted to dismiss his parents' objections from my mind. I threw myself into planning our wedding. For reasons known only to them, the Wellingtons did attend the ceremony. They even gave us a wedding gift—a sterling silver tea service.

"We need this like a hole in the head," I remarked later to my new husband. "When would I ever use such a thing?" Alden had refused any financial help from his family, and his salary at the bank where he worked only allowed us to rent a small, cheap apartment.

"It does stand out like a sore thumb," he said as he chuckled. "However, maybe it means Mother and Dad are coming around."

"When snow freezes in Hell," I said. I put the tea service on the top shelf of our bedroom closet.

The phone suddenly rang, chasing away my memories.

"Is everything okay, Suze?" It was my mother.

"Sure, Mom," I said. "Why are you calling me so early? It's still dawn."

Mom was never one to mince words. "Honey, if you'd rather your father and I didn't come, we'll understand."

I glanced at the small table in our living room. The night before, I'd spent hours trying to make it look pretty. My mother had loaned me her white lace tablecloth, glass candleholders, and a centerpiece of fake autumn leaves she always used on Thanksgiving. I'd placed new yellow candles in the holders, but when I stood back to admire the effect, I realized the plastic plates, goblets, and stainless-steel cutlery detracted from the impression I'd wished to impart. The only expensive item in view was the sterling silver teapot, sugar, and creamer. I'd retrieved it from the closet and set it at the end of the kitchen counter.

"Why would you ask that, Mom?" I asked. "Of course, you must come. I've already set the table for six."

"I was thinking of the Wellingtons," she replied. "Having to deal with them is enough without having to please us, too."

"Oh, they're not so bad anymore," I lied. "They actually talk to me now . . . sorta. I can handle it."

"Are you sure?"

"Just come, Mom. If the Wellingtons act rudely, you and Daddy can put them in their place."

"I've wanted to do that for ages," my mother admitted. "But how can you convince a woman money isn't everything? I swear, Suze, sometimes I think the woman isn't even human."

I faked a laugh. "You've nailed Alden's mother down to a tee. Now let me get to the turkey."

"If you say so, honey." I could hear the doubt still reflected in my mother's voice. "We'll see you at six o'clock."

Both sets of parents arrived at the same time, and I was effusive, pasting a wide smile on my face and making welcoming sounds while Alden took their coats and hung them in the closet.

"Where shall we sit, Suze?" my father asked as he looked at our one couch.

"At the table, Daddy. The turkey finished cooking early."

"No predinner cocktails?" Mrs. Wellington asked and disapproval colored her words.

"We have wine to drink with the meal," Alden replied. "Sit down, Mother."

He led each parent to his or her respective places.

"The table looks beautiful, Suze," my mother said. "I love the yellow candles; they match some of the leaves in the centerpiece."

"Thanks, Mom," I answered, and my heart sank as I watched Alden's mother observe everything with a look of distaste. With her manicured fingernails, she tapped the plates and goblets. Was she going to comment and say that plastic was tacky?

Alden must have read my mind, because he immediately started pouring the wine.

"Pretty good stuff," his father remarked, tasting the red liquid. "What is it?"

"Imported red wine."

"You're supposed to serve white wine with poultry." Alden's mother sniffed, and she stared directly at me. She obviously believed I was the person who committed this social gaffe.

"What difference does it make?" Mom asked, running her tongue delicately over her lips. "It's delicious."

"A toast," my father announced, raising his glass. "To our happily married children, who have allowed us to share their first Thanksgiving with them."

Everyone nodded, and drained their goblets. While Alden quickly did refills, I retreated to the kitchenette behind them, and started serving the meal.

"Can I help you, Suze?" Mom asked.

"No, Alden will," I answered. "You drink your wine. This might take a few moments."

Our parents were on their third serving when I finally assembled the food on the table. In spite of the presence of the Wellingtons, I felt confident that I'd cooked a presentable feast. The mashed potatoes were snowy, the carrots had caramelized to a perfect golden color, there were no lumps in my gravy, the rolls were hot, and the tray of raw relishes to accompany the food was a masterpiece.

When I brought in the turkey, Mrs. Wellington raised her

eyebrows. "How much does that bird weigh?" she asked, staring at the crusty brown skin oozing juices.

"Thirty pounds." I set the turkey in front of Alden, who carved the meat into slices and placed them on a serving platter. When he finished, I removed the bird, and everyone began passing the food around.

"Gracious, Suze, I never cooked such a huge turkey," my mother said, her words slightly slurred. Mom wasn't used to drinking—especially on an empty stomach.

"I hope it's not raw," Mrs. Wellington said. "You can become violently ill if poultry isn't fully cooked."

I wanted to strangle her, but instead I smiled. "I put it in the oven at dawn," I assured her.

"It's a magnificent bird," Alden's father said, and to my surprise, smiled back at me. Evidently, he was feeling the effects of the wine also.

There were a few minutes of silence while everyone filled his or her plates.

"Let's say grace." My mother bowed her head. We followed her lead as we listened to the beautiful Thanksgiving prayer while the steaming dinner waited.

After the Amens, I held my breath as I watched my guests put a forkful of turkey into their mouths. I'd put a lot of work into my meal. Silently, I sent off a quick prayer that everything I'd cooked would be delicious.

"Ugh," Alden's father gurgled while his wife choked.

"What's the matter?" I looked at my husband, who was manfully attempting to swallow something which obviously tasted terrible.

"Suze—" my mother began, but couldn't finish. She turned aside and spit into her paper napkin while my father's face turned red.

"It can't be raw," I protested, and took a bite of the meat. My taste buds immediately rebelled at the bitterness, which filled my mouth.

"What's wrong with it?" I gasped.

Mom reached across the table and patted my hand. "Suze, dear, the turkey came fully dressed, did it not?"

"Yes, the cavity was empty except for the giblets if that's what you mean."

"Sweetheart, you didn't check it thoroughly. The butcher overlooked the gall bladder, and it probably burst in the oven. What you're tasting is bile, which has permeated the entire bird."

I'd put everything I had into planning and cooking this meal to impress the Wellingtons, and my dinner was ruined! I wanted to cry, but defiantly held back my tears.

"We can always eat the vegetables," Alden said brightly.

I just sat there, waiting for Mrs. Wellington to heap insults on my head. This was her opportunity to prove how unworthy I was to deserve her son. Only a dumb idiot from the lower class would make such a mistake.

"It rarely happens that they leave in the . . . ahem . . . gall bladder," Alden's father said. Then suddenly, he burst into laughter.

I looked up. Both of Alden's parents were giggling hysterically.

Were they going to make fun of me, too? I bit my quivering lip.

"Now, now, dear, it does happen occasionally." I couldn't believe that I was hearing Mrs. Wellington's voice. She turned to her husband. "Remember?"

He instantly started to laugh again.

"I'm . . . sorry," I murmured.

"Don't be, Suze. It's not your fault," Alden's mother soothed. "The same thing happened to me."

"It did?"

All of us listened intently as she continued. "It was our first Christmas, and I did exactly what you did. I wanted to impress my in-laws so I invited them to a turkey dinner at our home. Foolishly, I insisted on doing all the cooking myself." She looked at her husband. "We'd dismissed all the servants for the day including the cook?"

"Yes, we did," he answered, and reached for his wine.

"Anyway, the butcher left the gall bladder in my bird, too, and the turkey was inedible. I was positively humiliated. I bawled like a baby."

"Your grandmother almost fainted," Alden's father added. "We had to bring her smelling salts."

"It was dreadful," Mrs. Wellington said. "I've never cooked a turkey again." To my surprise, she pushed the turkey away from the rest of the food on her plate, and added, "I suggest we feast on the rest of this wonderful meal you prepared. Everything else looks and smells delicious."

"Thank-you for sharing your story with me," I said. "It makes me feel better."

"Yum, these carrots are superb, Suze." Mrs. Wellington smiled. "You must give my cook your recipe."

"It's actually Mom's recipe," I replied, and I looked at my mother, who winked at me.

"No matter whose it is, I simply must have it. And Suze, speaking of Mom's, I think it's time you begin calling me Mother. I cried buckets when my bird was ruined, but you haven't shed a tear. You have backbone, my girl."

I felt as though a great weight was lifted from my shoulders. I stole a glance at my husband who was grinning from ear to ear.

"You can call me Dad, Suze," Alden's father added gruffly. "I've always wanted a daughter."

"You never told me that," my husband said from the end of the table.

"Oh, hush, Son, and pour me another dash of that fabulous wine."

That thanksgiving was a turning point in my relationship with my in-laws. My mother-in-law is still not as warm as my own mother, but she has become friendlier. And, for that, I'm thankful.

THE END

HOLIDAY CHEER
You're Never Too Old For Thanksgiving

"I think you should go to the senior center for Thanksgiving dinner," my friend, Janice, suggested. "That way you won't be alone."

What Janice and all my friends didn't understand was that I could be in a group of a thousand people and I'd still feel alone without Barry at my side. It had been a year since my husband had died of a sudden heart attack and I still felt his absence everywhere I went.

I fought back tears, remembering the holidays we'd spent together over the forty-eight years of our marriage. He won't be with me this year, or ever again.

I swallowed my tears and forced a smile to my face. "I'll fix a small dinner for myself," I argued. "I like turkey and it makes great leftovers. Besides, all the stores have turkeys on sale for the holidays."

Janice gave a small sigh. "It's just too bad that I'm not having dinner at my house this year."

"Don't worry about me," I said. "Thanksgiving is only one day of the year and I'll be perfectly fine by myself."

As I said the words, I knew how wrong they were. Thanksgiving itself may only be one day, but it heralded in the holiday season loaded with fun-filled activities for families and couples.

I'd been in such a daze the previous year with Barry's sudden passing that I hadn't even noticed the holiday activity all around me. But this year I'd already heard Christmas carols and saw decorated trees in the stores, as well as noticing merchants setting up Christmas tree lots. The holidays are for children and couples, not for seventy-year-old widows. I may be fine by myself, but I would be lonely.

I pointedly looked at my watch. "It's time we got back to the reception desk," I said as I slid my chair away from the table.

Janice and I both volunteer at St. Mary's hospital several days a week. Our usual assignment was to work at the reception desk, answer questions, and direct visitors around the large hospital.

As we walked past the emergency room, I couldn't help glancing through the glass doors and remembering Barry lying so quietly on the stretcher as the doctors and nurses fought to save his life. My eyes had willed the straight line on the heart monitor to burst to life with heartbeats, but I already knew that no medical heroics could save him. I was a nurse before I'd retired and when Barry collapsed on the floor that morning I knew from his vital signs and lack of response to CPR that he'd already left me.

I pulled my thoughts back to the present and mentally started preparing a shopping list for my Thanksgiving dinner. I'd get a turkey and fix a whole meal. Why not? I love to cook and I hadn't had turkey in ages.

A crisp November wind tousled my hair as I walked across the senior center parking lot. As I'd expected there were plenty of vacant parking spots. Most people at the center spent Thanksgiving with their families. I'd firmly intended to prepare myself a turkey dinner and have lots of leftovers, like I'd told Janice. But when I got to the grocery store and saw the turkeys, I couldn't believe it. When had they gotten so big? I'd have leftovers for a lifetime if I cooked one of them.

I stood in the meat department wondering what to do when a woman walked by me with a basket overflowing with all of the essentials for a holiday meal. Suddenly, I was overwhelmed just thinking about cooking a turkey, chopping up vegetables for stuffing, and peeling potatoes just for me. I decided to go to the senior center after all. Maybe I'd see someone I knew, but I doubted it. Everyone I knew was with his or her families.

I was hanging my coat on the coat rack when a tall man with silver hair walked into the entryway. He gazed around the room before his eyes settled on me.

"I guess we hang our coats here," he said as followed my example and slipped off his navy blue wool coat.

I didn't come to the center often, but from the expression on his face and his actions I was sure he was a first-time visitor.

"I think they're serving dinner in the activity room," I said, pointing toward a brightly lit room used for large gatherings.

"Thanks," he said as he fell in step with me. "I've never been here before, but I couldn't resist the idea of a turkey dinner." He explained how he volunteers next door at the youth center and had seen a poster about the center's holiday meal.

We paid for our dinners and then walked through the serving line. I didn't recognize a person in the room. I wasn't in the mood to make conversation with strangers, so I headed for a small, empty table.

"Do you mind if I sit with you?" he asked.

"Please do," I said. I'd just as soon sit alone, but I didn't want to be rude. Obviously his circumstances were like mine and he was without a place to be. The least I could do was be polite.

"By the way, I'm Jerry Jackson," he said as he spread his napkin on his lap.

"Alice Turner," I said and gave him a smile.

Jerry is a pleasant looking man. He'd dressed for dinner in black wool slacks and a long-sleeve white shirt, open at the collar. With his silver hair and deep gray eyes he looked distinguished, yet very friendly.

"I like to cook," he said, "but turkey and stuffing are way beyond my skill level. I'm more of a steak and hamburger chef."

"Turkey is a lot of work for just one," I agreed as I remembered my recent trip to the grocery store.

He nodded. "My wife used to always cook a big meal, but she passed away a couple of years ago from breast cancer."

"I'm sorry," I said, understanding his loss all too well. "My husband died of a heart attack last year."

Jerry's gray eyes darkened and he gave me an understanding nod. "Do you have kids?"

"I have a daughter. She and her husband are spending the holiday with his family in Texas. How about you?"

"I've got two boys. One of them lives in Denver and the other one is serving in Iraq."

I looked up and met his gaze. "That has to be a worry."

"It is. I don't even watch the news anymore. I used to worry myself sick."

We talked about current events for a while, then the conversation drifted back to ourselves.

"You said that you volunteer next door?" I said.

"I'm a retired high school basketball coach," he explained. "When I retired I missed working with the kids, so I started coaching the boys at the youth center. How about you? What do you do?"

I told him about being at St. Mary's for my entire nursing career and how I'm a volunteer there.

"Sounds like we both keep busy."

I nodded.

"But the holidays can still be lonely even if a person is busy," he said. "There are things I like to do, like going to the town's tree lighting and concerts, but it's not much fun going alone. When I go with friends I often feel like a tag-along."

"That's true," I agreed as I thought about how much I like the holiday concerts. I'd even thought about going to the tree lighting, but had dismissed the idea because it wasn't much fun to go alone.

Jerry ran his finger around the lip of his cup, then looked up and met my gaze. "Don't get me wrong," he began. "You don't even know me, but if you'd like to go to some of the holiday events I'd be glad to accompany you. Actually, I'd welcome your company."

At first his suggestion shocked me, but I thought: Why not? Then I wondered about his motives. After all, he'd been a widower for two years.

"I'm not looking for a husband," I blurted out.

He smiled. "And I'm not looking for a wife. In fact, by this time next year I'll be living in Denver."

"You're moving?" Denver is a long ways away.

"I've decided to move closer to my son. Since Melinda died, there really isn't anything to keep me here. However, it may take some time to sell my house."

Our conversation drifted off to the economy and house sales. With Jerry we bounced from topic to topic, but neither of us lost track. Eventually we wound up back to talking about attending holiday events together.

"Would you like to do some holiday things together?" he asked again. "The tree lighting is tomorrow night."

What's the harm, I thought. We certainly have a lot to talk about. He seems like a nice man and he's not looking for a permanent commitment. "Sure," I agreed.

As I drove home from the senior center, I wondered if I'd lost my mind. I'd just agreed to spend an evening with a man that I'd known for less than a couple of hours. I quickly reminded myself that I was playing it safe and meeting him under the clock at the city center. But as safe as our meeting may be, it didn't feel right to be going out with a man other than Barry. It seemed dishonorable.

I wasn't cheating on Barry. I would never have done anything like that. I knew part of my discomfort was that I hadn't been in the company of any man other Barry for many years. I hadn't felt any discomfort sharing dinner with Jerry. We'd talked non-stop.

By the time I pulled into my driveway I'd convinced myself that seeing Jerry was perfectly acceptable behavior since we're both single. Besides, we'd agreed that neither of us had expectations of a grand romance.

My heart skipped a beat the next day when I spotted Jerry. I thought he looked distinguished the day before, but now he looked downright handsome. Worried about my unexpected reaction, I began to wonder if meeting him was a smart idea after all. Before I could act on my concerns, he waved hello and walked toward me.

"The program begins at eight o'clock," he said. "I thought we'd get something to eat at Murphy's and then walk around until it's time for the ceremony.

I agreed and we walked the short distance to Murphy's, a steak and barbecue place. As much as I enjoy talking with Janice, it's nice to have a male point of view on current events and other subjects.

It seemed like the waitress had just served our first course when she handed Jerry the check. I realized I should've told her to make separate checks. I was too new at this male-female friendship arrangement. Jerry quickly glanced at the charges, slipped his credit card into the plastic folder, and handed it back to the waitress.

"I want to pay my portion," I protested, taking my wallet from my purse.

"That's okay. I've got it covered," he said.

I shook my head. "We agreed to be friends. It's only right that I pay my share."

"Next time we'll do separate checks," he said.

I slipped my wallet back into my purse. I didn't feel comfortable about him paying for dinner, but at the moment it seemed the easiest way to handle the bill.

People of all ages, carrying shopping bags, drinking hot chocolate, and talking with friends, filled the plaza. We stopped at several vendors and looked at the holiday displays. Unlike many men, Jerry liked looking at them.

"How about a raffle ticket?" one of the vendors called out to us. "The grand prize is two tickets to The Nutcracker at the Performing Arts Center."

"I'll buy a ticket," Jerry said as he pulled out his billfold.

"Me, too."

"If I win, I'll take you," he said matter-of-factly.

"And if I win, I'll take you."

A local high school band and choir were performing when we arrived at the tree lighting area. We managed to find a good place to stand so we had a full view of the tree and the ceremonies.

"What color do you think the lights are this year?" Jerry asked.

The tree is lit in a different color scheme every year. I tried to remember the color last year, but then I didn't come down to the center. I'd been too depressed and hardly left the house. Guilt tugged my heart. It didn't seem right to be there, enjoying myself without Barry. But, I quickly reminded myself that I was doing nothing wrong. I'm now a single woman and it was okay to be with Jerry.

"I'll bet they're multi-colored this year," I said.

"I'll go with white."

It turned out we were both wrong. Gold was this year's color. Jerry and I applauded as the mayor switched on the tree and a golden glow filled the night. The mayor then began drawing tickets for the raffle prizes. Jerry and I both studied our tickets as number after number was called and prizes were awarded for restaurant coupons, holiday flower arrangements, and other things. My breath caught in my throat when the mayor called my number for the grand prize.

"You won the Nutcracker tickets!" Jerry said, squeezing my arm as I jumped up down, waving my ticket in the air.

"It looks like we're going to the show," I said as I walked up to claim my prize.

"How about a buttered rum or glass of wine?" Jerry suggested as the ceremonies came to a close.

"That's a perfect way to celebrate my win," I agreed.

We found a table in a nearby bar and ordered drinks. When the waitress delivered them I immediately grabbed the check and paid the bill.

"I'm paying for our celebration."

"The Nutcracker is my favorite holiday play," Jerry said as he stirred his buttered rum. "We'll have to have dinner before the show."

I felt like a teenager as we made plans for our night out. It had been a long, long time since I'd been excited about going anywhere. I was glad that I'd gone to the senior center. This arrangement with Jerry was going to make the holidays so much more fulfilling and less lonely.

"You met a man!" Janice exclaimed on Monday when I told her about Jerry. We were having coffee and doughnuts in the hospital cafeteria before reporting for duty at the reception desk.

"He's not a boyfriend," I said, waving away the gleam in her eyes.

"But you like him," she argued.

"Of course I do. Why else would I want to spend time with him?"

"Maybe this will lead to something more permanent," she suggested.

I shook my head. "We both agreed that we're not planning to remarry," I explained. "Besides, Jerry is moving to Denver."

"Oh," she said in a disappointed tone.

"Janice, you know that I'm not looking for a husband."

"That's what Audrey said and look what happened to her. She and Don are celebrating their second anniversary next month."

Audrey is one of our friends who lost her husband to cancer and vowed that she'd never get married again. Less than a year after her husband had died, she started dating Don. As they say, the rest is history.

"Jerry has his house up for sale," I told her. "It's just a matter of time before it sells."

Janice dusted doughnut sugar from her hands and met my gaze. "Then just be sure you watch your feelings so you don't get hurt when he leaves."

"My feelings won't get hurt," I assured her. "We're just two people who don't like to go to do holiday activities alone or be a third wheel with other couples."

"When are you going to the Nutcracker?" she asked.

"Not for a couple of weeks. I probably won't see him before then."

I remembered my words hours later when my phone rang and Jerry was on the line.

"I was getting ready to head out to buy items for the Christmas box I'm putting together for Patrick and his troop in Iraq and I thought of you. I thought you might enjoy helping me pick out things to put in the box. And, frankly, I'd like the company. This kind of shopping is always more fun with someone else along."

Within seconds I'd agreed to meet him, with plans to shop and then have dinner in the shopping center.

As usual I had a wonderful evening with Jerry. I couldn't remember a more fun time shopping. We walked through the aisles loading Jerry's basket with all kinds of toiletry and snack items before we arrived at the book section, where we wound up discussing our favorite authors and even buying books for ourselves, too. The evening was topped off with a bottle of Chianti and chicken Parmesan.

"Sounds to me like you're dating," Janice said the next day at the hospital.

I shook my head. "I probably won't see him again until The Nutcracker." But I was wrong.

Saturday morning I'd just filled my slow cooker with beef stew ingredients when Jerry called.

"How would you like a Christmas tree?"

He went on to explain that he and the boys from the youth center had cut Christmas trees and they had an extra one.

"The boys are helping me decorate mine right now. I could drop your tree off late this afternoon."

I hadn't even thought about getting a tree. Well, I'd thought about it but had dismissed the idea. Setting up a tree seemed like too much work just for me.

"I'll put it in the stand and help with the lights," he offered.

"You're welcome to stay for dinner and decorate the tree," I said as I glanced at the slow cooker that was just beginning to bubble. I'd made enough stew for a couple of meals; no reason I couldn't share with him. I gave Jerry directions to my house, and then went into the attic to get my Christmas decorations.

I opened the first box and tears caught in my throat immediately. As I held a crystal bell that Barry and I had bought on one our trips to the beach, I pictured his smile and deep blue eyes. I even imagined the scent of him with his musky cologne and special soap that he used every morning.

I picked up another ornament and memories again filled my heart. Tears were streaming down my checks by the time I opened the last box. I cried even harder as I remembered intimate moments when Barry would hold me in his arms and kiss me until I thought my heart would burst with love.

I sat on the floor among the boxes, wiping my eyes with the back of my hand. It didn't feel right that a man other than Barry was going to help decorate my tree and sit at my dining room table. Granted I'm a widow, but it seemed wrong. Yet, I enjoyed being with Jerry. It's only temporary for the holidays, I reminded myself, since Jerry is moving to Denver.

I was still teary-eyed when the phone rang. I stumbled to my feet and climbed down the attic stairs. I caught the phone right before it went to voice mail.

"Are you all right?" my daughter asked when I gave a teary, breathy hello.

"Yes," I said. "I was in the attic and had to race to get the phone."

"We're decorating the tree tonight and I thought you'd like to come over for dinner and to help."

There was nothing I'd like better than spending an evening with Wanda and my grandkids, but Jerry was coming over. I groaned to myself, trying to figure out how to tell her about Jerry. She'd probably jump to conclusions like Janice and think I was dating. But I couldn't lie.

"So, you're seeing someone," Wanda said after I told her about Jerry.

"Not really," I explained again. "We're just friends."

"That's how relationships start," she said in a tone that was surprisingly lighthearted and happy. I thought she'd feel I was being disloyal to her father if I ever considered dating. I was stunned that she sounded like my seeing Jerry was a good thing.

"Wouldn't you be upset if I dated someone?" I asked.

"No, I'd probably be happy," she said matter-of-factly. "Assuming he's a nice man, of course, and treated you right. I know it's got to be lonely without Dad now. If you can find someone to make you happy, then you need to follow your heart."

While I was confused about my own feelings, I was proud that my daughter was open-minded and cared about my happiness. But I had to set her straight.

"I'm not planning on having a relationship with Jerry," I explained. "He's going to be moving to Denver."

"That's too bad. It sounds like you get along really well and you like being with him."

I hauled my boxes down from the attic after we hung up. As I worked, I thought how crazy it was that Janice and Wanda were so gung-ho for me to have a relationship when it was the furthest thing from my mind—although I had to admit that I did enjoy Jerry's company.

Every time we were together I liked him even more. I suppose if I were seriously interested in dating, Jerry would be the man I'd pick. He was certainly handsome. My heart gave a little flutter. We have a lot of common interests. But it was silly to be thinking this way. Jerry is moving and we're only seeing each other during the holidays.

"It's a beautiful tree," Jerry said as we stepped back and admired the noble fir that graced the corner of my living room. The lights sparkled like stars and the ornaments shimmered.

I nodded, suddenly choked with tears. This year's tree symbolized so much—the past memories of Barry; my life without Barry at my side; and celebrating the holidays with a male friend. I turned my gaze from the tree and faced Jerry. His eyes were filled with warmth and compassion.

"The tree probably makes you a little sad," he said softly. "I know that's how I felt last year when I put up a tree without Melinda. The tree was pretty with all the decorations we'd collected over the years, but the room felt empty without her to share it."

I nodded again, amazed at his insightfulness. "You're right. I suppose I'll be stronger next year."

"I think when you've had a good marriage, the person you lost is always in your heart," he said. "You can't help but think of them, especially at Christmas when holiday memories are so strong. But as time goes by, a person makes new memories. Or at least I have. The new memories don't erase the old; they just add to the experience of life."

I liked Jerry's philosophies. People often joke about men being shallow, but Jerry was anything but that. Perhaps losing his wife gave him depth or insight into people's feelings that many men don't have.

"How about opening the wine while I toss the salad?" I asked to lighten the mood.

We worked as though we'd shared the kitchen for years. I tossed the salad while he opened the bottle of Merlot and filled two glasses. Then he carried the pot of stew to the dining room table.

"My realtor called when the boys from the center and I were in the middle of decorating my tree," he said as he ladled stew into his bowl. "She wanted to show my house. I told her that it wasn't picture-perfect with my tree only partly decorated and storage boxes scattered all over the living room. But she said the couple was in her car and they wanted to see the house even if it was messy. I took the boys out for sundaes while the realtor showed the house. I was surprised at the call, since most people aren't house hunting this time of year."

"Maybe you'll get lucky and your house won't be on the market long," I said as I buttered a roll.

"Maybe," he said thoughtfully. "I'm going to Denver for a few weeks over Christmas to look at houses there."

With the talk of Jerry looking for houses, the fact that he would be moving suddenly felt real. A cold sense of loss spread through my bones when I thought about not seeing him again. Each time we were together I liked him even more.

Janice's warning about my not getting hurt when he moved away flashed through my mind. I hadn't thought my feelings would be a problem. But they could be, if I wasn't careful.

"What are you doing for Christmas?" he asked, interrupting my thoughts.

"I'll be at my daughter's. We're going to go to Christmas Eve services at her church and then having a turkey dinner on Christmas Day at her house."

"One of the boys at the youth center asked me to attend his church's holiday program. He's one of the soloists. If you'd like, you're welcome to come with me."

"I'd love to." So I had more plans to be with Jerry. It was becoming a habit that I liked all too much. I just had to be wary and keep my emotions in check.

"Would you like to have a nightcap?" Jerry suggested as we walked out of the Performing Arts Center. The Nutcracker performance had been beautiful, made even more enjoyable with Jerry at my side.

I hate to admit it, but when he touched me to take my coat at the theater, shivers of heat ran through my veins and a rush of desire rushed through me. My thoughts and feelings were anything but platonic.

I had to be realistic and face facts. He was leaving for Denver the next day to look for a house and to begin a new life. His realtor had told him that the people who'd looked at his house were putting together a good offer. By this time next month, Jerry could be settling in Denver. Until then I wanted to enjoy my time with him.

"A drink sounds nice," I agreed.

We both ordered buttered rum drinks and then started talking about the performance.

"Would you like another?" Jerry asked when the waitress came by.

As much as I longed to extend the evening, I shook my head. One drink was usually my limit and I knew Jerry had to get up early to catch his flight.

He nodded. "I guess we should get going if I have to be awake in the morning to make it to the airport on time."

Since it would probably be the last time that I saw him, I thought

I should let him know how much I'd enjoyed the past few weeks.

"Having your company was much better than going alone or being a tag-along. It was also nice to be with someone without having expectations for something other than friendship," I quickly added. They were awkward words, but the best I could come up with.

"I've enjoyed myself, too," he said thoughtfully.

Usually we communicated so well, but I felt like we were strangers struggling for words. Yet, what more was there to say?

The drive back to my house was unusually quiet. Of course, usually we talked about upcoming events and things we were going to do. I imagined that Jerry's mind was on last-minute packing while I was thinking I'd probably never see him again. I reminded myself once more that I knew seeing him would be temporary.

"I hope you have a wonderful holiday with your son and find the perfect house," I said when he walked me to my door.

"You have a nice holiday with your family, too." His gray eyes clouded a minute, and then he waved good night and walked to his car.

I stood behind the living room curtain watching the taillights of his car disappear into the night. It's been a wonderful month, I thought as I remembered all of the things we'd done. I just wish it didn't have to end.

"I warned you about falling in love with him," Janice said, giving me a sympathetic gaze across the cafeteria table at St. Mary's.

"I'm not in love," I protested. The fact that Jerry had been on my mind every moment since he left me at my door after The Nutcracker didn't mean I was in love. But it was a sign that he'd become more than just a casual friend or an escort to holiday events. I may not be in love yet, but I knew that my emotions were heading in that direction.

"I guess what happened with Jerry took me by surprise," I admitted. "I didn't think I could develop feelings for another man. When Barry died, I planned to live alone for the rest of my life."

"But then you met Jerry," she said softly and smiled.

I nodded. Memories flashed through my mind, warming my heart and soul. At the same time they made my heart ache, knowing I wouldn't be seeing Jerry again. It was more than just going places with him. I genuinely liked him and cared about him.

"Life is much more enjoyable with someone to share it with," I said. "When we first started seeing each other I felt like I was being disloyal to Barry. But I know if I'd died first, I wouldn't want Barry to be lonely. I'd understand if he found someone to be with."

"I'm sure Barry would feel the same way about you. Too bad things didn't work out with Jerry. He sounded like a good match for you. But now you know that you would be open to romance again."

While I agreed with her, I wasn't ready to join a singles' club.

When, and if, there was a man for me, I'd meet him in the course of daily living like I met Jerry.

Later that night I was fixing dinner for myself when the phone rang. I nearly dropped the handset when I heard Jerry's voice.

"I'm at the Denver airport on my way home."

"You're leaving early?" Jerry had planned to be in Denver until after New Year's.

"I need to sign some papers at the realtor's. Besides, I'm done here."

"So the house hunting went well?"

"I'll tell you all about it when I see you. I was hoping we could get together tomorrow night, but I know finding a restaurant on New Year's Eve will be impossible."

"I can fix us dinner," I suggested.

"I'll bring a bottle of wine and we can toast the New Year." I could feel his smile through the phone.

My heart bounced with joy as I hung up the phone. Jerry is coming to dinner tomorrow night! As quickly as my feelings soared they crashed to the ground. He's coming to tell me all about the house that he found miles from here. The deal on his house in town must have gone through or he wouldn't need to see his realtor to sign papers. Tomorrow night will be a mixed blessing.

The doorbell rang and my heart leaped to my throat, beating like it would never stop. "Jerry is my friend and nothing more," I softly said to myself as I walked to the door.

I took a deep breath and opened the door. Our gazes met and locked and it was all I could do not to wrap my arms around him.

Instead I said, "Come on in."

I tried to ignore his sexy appearance, warm eyes, and happy smile as I hung up his coat. Just looking at him made my heart race and my body tingle.

"What's for dinner?" he asked. "It smells wonderful."

"Chicken cacciatore," I said. "Would you like dinner now, or would you like to have a glass of wine and tell me about your house hunting?"

"Let's have some wine."

I checked the cacciatore while he pulled the cork and poured us each a glass of Merlot. He held his glass up to mine and we touched glasses, sending a ring of crystal into the air.

"To the New Year," he said.

"To the New Year," I repeated, unable to come up with anything else to say. "The deal on your house here must have gone through since you had papers to sign," I said as I sat down at one end of the sofa and he sat at the other end.

"The couple who saw the house before Christmas made a great offer, more than I'd expected."

"That's wonderful," I said. I was so happy for him, but I knew it meant that was the last time I'd see him.

"But I turned it down and signed papers to take my house off the market."

I gave him a puzzled look. "You didn't find a house in Denver that you liked?"

"I saw all kinds of nice houses," he said. "Many were at great prices." He paused and met my gaze. "But every time I looked at a house, I thought of you."

My breath caught and I swallowed hard, not believing my ears.

"At Thanksgiving I thought we'd attend a few holiday events together and enjoy the holidays," he said. "But for me, it's turning into something more. A lot more. I enjoy our time together and I look forward to being with you. When you're not around I miss you."

"I thought of you every day when you were in Denver," I said softly, hardly able to speak.

His eyes brightened and his lips curled into a smile. "You did?"

I nodded. "I missed you so much."

"We've only known each other a few weeks, but in my heart I couldn't move away without getting to really know you and see where our friendship will go. Life has taught me that special people and relationships only come along a few times in life. I don't want to miss this opportunity."

"I'm happy that you're staying," I said. "I feel the same way."

"We've got lots of holidays to get to know each other," he joked. "February is full of them. There's Lincoln's Birthday, Washington's birthday, and Valentine's Day." He gave me a sexy grin that made me blush to my toes.

It took all the restraint in my bones not to throw myself into his arms and hug him. I decided to throw caution to the wind. "Do I have to wait until midnight for a New Year's Eve kiss?" I asked.

"Oh, I think we should practice now," he said as scooted across the sofa and took me into his arms.

THE END

GOBBLEZILLA TAKES A BOW

"Alexa, you've got to come out, honey," Theodore said. "It's not that big a deal."

I stared out the bedroom window. My throat felt so raw from crying I couldn't have answered him if I'd wanted. Why in the world did my husband want me out of the bedroom? If I were Theodore, I'd not only leave me in my room, but I'd skip the country.

It was supposed to be such a special occasion. Everyone took turns hosting family get-togethers. This was my sister-in-law's (she was married to Ted's brother) turn, but her baby was due at any day. So I volunteered to have the celebration at our apartment. I wanted to do it for them, to feel part of their family. Now I'd ruined it, made a fool of myself, and probably alienated Theodore's family forever. After six months of marriage, I was a complete failure. I'd tried so hard to make everything perfect. Studying every cookbook available, I planned and planned. I'm good at planning, or so I thought. In addition to his family, I'd invited some neighbors and people from work. When anyone offered to bring a dish, I made such a big deal about consulting my "Master Menu List," I turned them down. This was to be my production and my production alone.

Once or twice, my mother-in-law started to suggest something. But I was so determined to do this myself, I'd wave that stupid Master List and announce, "I have it under control!"

Theodore joked about my buying a turkey big enough to feed the multitude I'd invited. It was so huge it wouldn't fit in our refrigerator freezer. Eventually I found a friend who let me store it in their deep freezer. The television commercial where everyone warned the others that the turkey would be "too dry" made me paranoid. I bought a hypodermic needle to baste that turkey inside out. Those syringes now sat like a surgeon's tools on my kitchen cabinet, one of them bent.

Theodore had fussed about how much the dinner was starting to cost. He kept asking, "Why don't you talk to my mother about the menu? This is supposed to be a family gathering, not a state banquet. We don't have that kind of money!"

Everyone knows that mentioning Mama or Mama doing something well, are the last words that any husband should say to a new wife. It's like a red flag in front of a bull, except I wasn't a bull, just bullheaded. No way did I want to talk to his mother. Besides, I worked hard for our money, too. I wanted this to be a perfect family dinner.

I was able to use all the pretty dishes I'd received as wedding presents. They were in the kitchen, ready to use first thing this morning. I'd even made the relish trays ahead of time. Everything was ready when I asked Theodore to put the turkey in the oven for me. It took both him and his father to load the turkey in the oven. Theodore's dad dubbed it "Gobblezilla." They picked it up and started to push it in. It wouldn't fit.

I could still hear Theodore's mother saying, "Oh, my." I figured she wanted to finish the sentence, "Oh my stupid daughter-in-law."

"Maybe we can put it on a lower rack," my sister-in-law suggested.

"It is on the lower rack," Theodore grumbled. "How much does this bird weigh, anyway, Alexa?"

All eyes looked at me. I turned to one of our neighbors. "Is your oven big enough?"

"The apartments all have the same size ovens, Alexa," she answered. Theodore's parents looked at one another. "We can try ours," his dad offered. "It's just a few minutes across town. We'll shove this baby in and drive it back when it's ready."

"I can't leave everyone," I protested.

"Mom can do it," Theodore said glibly.

My self-confidence crumbled. His entire family already thought I was an idiot. His mom would make the perfect turkey, and everyone would be relieved she had done it instead of Theodore's ditzy bride. As a sort of parting gift, I decided to go ahead and use a syringe on it. Pulling the plunger back, I filled the vial with melted butter. I slapped it into the turkey, just as an experienced nurse did with a patient. Only the needle wouldn't go in.

I pushed and pushed and it wouldn't budge. "It won't go in," I hissed at Theodore. He pushed on it harder and that's when it bent. "Alexa, it's frozen solid," he said. "When did you take it out to thaw?"

"Yesterday," I answered, indignant that he'd think I'd only taken it out that morning.

"Alexa, even I know it needs to be in the refrigerator a couple a days to thaw. Gobblezilla here probably needed a week! I can't believe you could be so stup—"

"Theodore!" His mother's tone was one I'd heard only one other time to reprimand her grown children. Instead of being grateful, for her stopping him, I felt totally humiliated that my mother-in-law would have to defend me. The tears burned my eyes as I ran out of the room to the bedroom. I felt like running out of the apartment and out of Theodore's life. I wished with all my heart that his CD were playing louder so I could sob into my pillow instead of merely having to whimper.

80

By the time he came to the door, I'd actually fallen asleep. I'd been up very late getting everything ready and awakened very early to prepare the food. Instead of a perfect dinner, I'd created a mess. All of my plans were ruined. If I couldn't cook a turkey, why did I think I could make a marriage work?

Glancing at the clock, I realized it had been an hour since I fled the scene of my crime. All eyes would be on me if I returned, but it didn't matter. My marriage was over anyway.

No one seemed to notice when I walked down the hall. The guys and a lot of women were watching pregame chatter on the television. The dining room table was set beautifully, and I could have sworn I smelled cooking turkey. When I walked to the kitchen, I heard a timer beep, just in time to see my mother-in-law peek into the oven.

"Looks ready to me. Let's put it on Alexa's pretty platter."

I felt as if I were in a dream watching my mother-in-law and neighbor pulled a big aluminum tray out of the oven and fork sliced turkey onto the platter. As I glanced at the waste can in the corner, I saw a huge ready-to-eat frozen entree box. Everyone gathered around the table, grumbling good-naturally about how hungry they were.

Theodore came up and put his arms around my shoulders. "Ready to eat?" he asked. He pulled out a chair for me, as if I was a queen or something. His father cleared his throat just as he did.

"I know this is my son's house, but I'd like to dedicate the meal to a marriage—mine."

All eyes turned to my in-laws.

"Thirty years ago my wife and I lived in a dump," he began. "She prepared her first Thanksgiving dinner in our apartment. We waited two hours before we realized the stove didn't work. I chastised my bride for being stupid and not checking to see if it worked before we bought the turkey. She told me I could go join the turkey as she threw it out the back door."

Several people laughed. Theodore squeezed my hand as his dad continued. "It was the beginning of two family traditions. The first was never ever to call my wife stupid. The second was TV dinners on Thanksgiving night. Alexa has no way of knowing this, but when most people are chowing down on leftovers Thanksgiving night, the wife and I share a TV dinner. It was my peace offering that day—and I've been thankful I've done it ever since."

"The dinners are better now," Theodore's mother said. "All they had back then were meat loaf and fried chicken and our little toaster oven didn't work that well."

Theodore's dad kissed me on the cheek. "So, Alexa, you've worked very hard on this meal that we'll enjoy. Theodore, you will be having humble pie for dessert while the rest of us enjoy pumpkin."

I smiled at my husband and his parents. Thirty years of happiness? I could live with that. Gobblezilla might even be thawed by then.

THE END

I wanted to show my family that I could
get a man on my own. So I showed up for
Thanksgiving dinner with

MY BLIND DATE FROM HELL

"**Y**ou're not getting any younger, Faith," Granny said when
I told her I still didn't have a special man in my life. "When are you
gonna settle down and start a family?"

She always asked me that, even when she'd seen me a day or
two before. It was almost as though Grandma thought that some man
would magically pop into my life and whisk me off on a white horse.
Even I'd given up on that fairy-tale notion years ago. . . .

"I don't know," I said with a sigh. "Just don't worry about it,
okay?"

"Listen to me, Faith," she said in a sharp tone. "If you don't hurry
up and meet Mr. Right soon, you'll be too old. Look at Mariella."

Mariella was my mother's sister, the "old maid" of the family, the
woman who'd never "snagged a man" and who'd live the rest of her
days alone. Never mind the fact that Mariella was the happiest woman
I'd ever met. She was the only one of Mom's siblings who had the
freedom to travel and the money to buy whatever she darn well pleased.

"Mariella seems perfectly content to me," I said. "I can't think of
anyone I'd rather be more like."

"Faith," she managed to growl out. "Don't give me that. Every
woman needs a good man in her life. Mariella's not nearly as happy
as she seems. Trust me on this."

By the time I got off the phone with Granny, I felt like pulling out
my hair. She never let up. It was a wonder Mariella still came around,
with Granny constantly nagging about her finding a man. However, I
knew Granny finally had given up on my aunt when I got to the point
she considered the "ripe age for marriage."

I told my best friend, Lorna, about Granny's nagging. She just
laughed when I explained to her how things would probably be during
the holidays. "Why don't you get one of the guys from your office
to pose as a date for Thanksgiving dinner to get her off your back?"
she asked.

With a shrug, I replied, "They're all either married or have plans
for Thanksgiving."

Lorna put her index finger on her chin, rolled her eyes up toward
the ceiling, and let out a breath. "Let's see," she said. "I just happen to

know someone who doesn't have any plans for Thanksgiving."

"Oh, no you don't, Lorna," I said as I backed away from my friend. "One matchmaker is all I can handle."

Lorna glared at me as if she was talking to a clueless child. "I'm not trying to play matchmaker, Faith. I'm just trying to help you out here. Your grandmother won't leave you alone about finding a man, and a nice man I know doesn't have plans for the holiday. He'll be alone in a town where he doesn't know a soul."

"Then why don't you invite him to go with you?" I asked.

Lorna and her boyfriend had plans to go to a cabin in the mountains for the long weekend. Both of their families lived on the other side of the continent, so they had their own special celebration.

She grinned at me and said, "Get real, Faith."

"Okay, so tell me about this guy," I finally said. "Why is he having such a hard time meeting people in this town where women outnumber the men two-to-one?"

"I think he's a little reserved," she replied.

"Reserved?"

I was almost blown over by her breath of exasperation. "Okay, so he's shy. You got a problem with that?"

"No, not really," I said after a brief pause. "But what else is wrong with him?"

"Well, I don't really know him all that well," she said, her voice at an uncomfortable pitch. Something else was going on here.

"How do you happen to know he doesn't have a place to go for Thanksgiving?" I prodded.

"We were both checking our mail, and when he couldn't get his key to turn, we started talking."

"His key?" I asked. Lorna had a very bad habit of talking around things until she decided to zero in on a point.

"Yeah, all it needed was a little oil. Anyway, after I oiled the lock in his mailbox, I asked him how he liked it here. We stood out in the lobby and chatted for about fifteen minutes."

"You learned about his loneliness in a fifteen-minute conversation?" I said. "Interesting."

"Actually, Brian's a very sweet man. He's from the Midwest, and he misses his family very much."

"That's nice," I said. "A man who misses his family."

"I think it's sweet," Lorna said. "At least he's not a jerk like most of the other single guys in this town."

Lorna was right. Most of the men I'd dated had been jerks, which was the precise reason I was still single. And I was perfectly happy.

"Okay," I finally conceded. "Tell me more about this Brian person."

She told me that Brian was a manufacturer's sales rep with a new territory in our area. He was in his late twenties, and he was nice looking but not what Lorna would call a "hunk," which was okay because that meant he wouldn't keep looking for a mirror. I'd had it with good-looking men who couldn't take their eyes off themselves, flexing their muscles when they didn't think I was looking.

"So, Faith," she said once she was finished telling me everything she knew about Brian. Amazing how it had taken her an hour to tell me what she'd learned in fifteen minutes. "Wanna take a chance?"

With a chuckle, I shrugged and replied, "Yeah, why not? What can happen during an afternoon at my grandmother's house?"

"Probably not much," Lorna said. "Not unless you and Brian fall in love and decide to make your grandmother a happy woman."

"Not a chance."

Lorna told me she'd knock on Brian's door later, and we could go from there. She was pretty sure he'd accept the Thanksgiving date, since he still didn't know anyone in town, from what she could tell. I told Lorna to call me and let me know where to be and when to be there. But deep down I really wasn't looking forward to meeting anyone. Most of my blind dates had turned out to be friends later, or they'd been disasters. Not one of them had turned into a hot romance.

Lorna called me the very next day. "I've made arrangements for the two of you to meet," she told me with excitement.

"Oh yeah?" I said. "Where?"

"Your place."

"My place?" Somehow, I thought we'd get together at Lorna's apartment, but oh, well.

"Yeah, your place."

"When?" I said as I picked up a pen to write it on my calendar.

"Uh, Thursday morning," she replied.

I dropped the pen. "Thursday morning? That's Thanksgiving."

"That's right," she said. "And Brian told me he'd love to go to your folks' house for Thanksgiving."

"You didn't invite him already, did you, Lor?" I screeched. "I figured we'd meet first, and then I'd decide if I wanted to bring him to Granny's."

"I didn't have a choice, Faith. He was busy up until then. Said his company has him hopping all over the place."

"Hopping?" I asked.

She nodded. "Like a bunny."

I let out the breath I just realized I'd been holding. What I really wanted to do was throttle Lorna, but I kept my cool.

"Well, I suppose that's all right. Brian can come here, then we can go on over to Granny's place." I'd deal with Lorna later.

85

"Should I tell him to bring something?" she asked.

"That might be a good idea," I replied. "I hate to show up empty-handed when I have dinner at someone's house."

"Okay, I'll leave a note on his door," she said.

"Brian better be nice, Lorna," I said.

"Nice?" she said, her voice squeaking. "He's nice—just don't expect some gorgeous hunk. I told you, he's just sort of cute."

"Lorna," I growled.

"I never said he was handsome, did I?"

"Well, no, you didn't say that."

"Okay, then, just accept Brian for who he is and try to have a good time with him," Lorna advised me. "Brian knows he's doing you a favor by going as a decoy."

"You didn't tell him that, did you?" I hissed.

"Well," she said, dragging out the word. "Yeah, sort of. . . ."

"Okay, okay, that's fine. But if this turns out to be a disaster, I might never forgive you."

"Don't say that, Faith. Brian's nice."

On Thanksgiving morning, I woke up bright and early. I'd promised to bring potato salad and a cherry pie, and I hadn't even started either one of them. I was in the kitchen working on them when I heard someone knocking at my door. It had to be Brian.

When I opened the door, there was a very pleasant looking, although not what I'd call "handsome" man around my age standing there, holding a casserole dish, and looking a bit sheepish. "Are you Brian?" I asked.

He nodded, smiled, and said, "And you must be Faith."

I took a step back. "C'mon in. I'm finishing up with my part of the dinner. Have a seat, and I'll be right out."

At least he isn't as unattractive as I feared he might be, I thought. Based on how Lorna had described him, he could have looked like a space creature. No, he really wasn't a hot-looking hunk, but he wasn't bad to look at.

Once the cherry pie was cool enough to handle and the potato salad was garnished, I carefully placed them into a box, covered it, and carried it out to the living room, where Brian sat patiently waiting. He'd picked up one of my magazines and was thumbing through it.

"Don't tell me you believe all these lies, Faith," he said, pointing to the article about how to please a man.

"Some of it's good stuff," I said, defending my choice of reading material.

He snickered and shook his head. "Give me a remote control, a beer, and a girlie magazine, and I'm set."

I thought he was kidding, so I laughed.

We chatted all the way to Granny's. Since Brian said his company car was in the shop, we took a cab, which suited me just fine.

"Lorna says your family's trying to get you married off," he blurted.

Lorna has a big mouth, I thought. I smiled at Brian, in spite of the thoughts going through my head about what I planned to do to Lorna later. "They want me to settle down," I replied.

He raised and lowered his eyebrows in a suggestive way. "Why, Faith? Are you a wild woman?"

Brian's look made my skin crawl. "No!" I said brusquely. "I'm not wild. I'm just not into relationships." There. That should hold him off—especially if he has any notions of this thing between him and me going any further.

"Want me to lay it on thick in front of your family?" he asked, apparently not fazed by my outburst.

"Thick?" I said, wanting clarification.

"Yeah. I can snuggle up to you and let them think we're hot for each other."

"That's really not necessary," I informed him. "Just be friendly. Be yourself."

He chuckled. I cringed.

What was I thinking when I'd accepted this blind date? If he hadn't brought what appeared to be a covered dish to share, I would have suggested dropping him off at his place on the way to Granny's.

She was waiting at the door for us when we arrived. Her eyes darted back and forth between Brian and me. Then she broke into a grin. "I'm so glad you brought your boyfriend, Faith," she whispered to me. Then she turned to Brian. "Better be nice to my granddaughter, or I'll put the curse on you."

As soon as Granny turned her back, Brian mouthed, "The curse?"

I nodded and whispered, "Yeah, she saw that in a movie once, and now she uses it."

"Oh," he replied, nodding as if he wasn't sure what to think.

Granny directed Brian to the living room where the men were watching sports on one of the cable channels. I joined the other women in the kitchen. No matter how good or bad of a cook the woman was, Granny insisted we do things her way. "It's tradition for the women to gather in the kitchen," she said.

I kind of liked hanging out with all the women, though, since it was the only time of year when we were all in the same room. Our chatter went from favorite recipes to Mariella's lack of a man in her life. She didn't seem to mind the attention being focused on her, though. In fact, she laughed right along with the rest of us.

Then Granny nodded toward me. "Faith finally snagged herself a man."

All heads turned toward me. Since Granny was the only one of the women who'd seen him, she felt it her duty to give a rundown on Brian.

"He's not all that great in the looks department, but I'm sure he has some other redeeming qualities," Granny said with her usual honesty.

"Tell us about him," Mariella said, her eyes twinkling with mischief. I wanted to pull her to the side and tell her it was all a farce, but I couldn't.

"Well, he's new to the area, and he's from the Midwest." I worked hard trying to remember the details about Brian, but I soon ran out of things to say.

"He's probably a very nice boy," Granny said. "Go tell the men it's almost time to eat."

Granny had used all the leaves to the dining room table that comfortably seated twelve, so all sixteen of us could eat together. Brian and I were practically sitting in each other's laps.

"Turkey?" Mariella asked as she passed one of the oval platters our way.

Brian shook his head, a look of disgust on his face. "How can you do that to such an innocent animal?"

"Huh?" Mariella scrunched up her nose and stared at him.

"Turkeys are the innocent victims at Thanksgiving, and I'm appalled by it," Brian went on. Then he went into a long monologue about how animals are raised only to be consumed by greedy humans. I watched as each person seated at the table began to lose their appetites.

Since Brian was my guest, though, I decided it was my job to liven things up at the table. "Well, you gotta try my sister's squash casserole. If you like vegetables, you'll love this."

Brian took one bite of it, then spit it out. My sister's face fell.

"What's wrong?" she asked, her voice low and squeaky. "Don't you like it?"

Brian shook his head. "Where's the squash? All I taste is Worcestershire sauce and bread crumbs."

Granny made a clicking sound with her false teeth, which let me know she was almost at the end of her rope. With a tight jaw, she passed him the mashed potatoes and hissed, "Have some potatoes, Brian. There's nothing in them but potatoes, a little cream, and some butter. And if that bothers you, the kitchen's that way." She pointed her finger toward the door behind him.

Brian nodded as he scooped out a mound of potatoes, which he dug into with gusto. I could tell he liked them by the way he took seconds, thirds, and then fourths. Everyone watched him scarf down massive quantities of Granny's white, fluffy potatoes.

"Pass me some more wine, Granny," Brian said, his mouth still full of potatoes.

Granny's eyebrows shot up at the fact that he'd taken liberties by calling her "Granny." But she didn't say anything. She just passed him the wine.

He kept the bottle by his side, pouring more when his glass was only half full. All he had during the main part of the meal were mashed potatoes and wine, and I could see that everyone else had noticed, too.

Suddenly, Brian jumped up from the table. "I almost forgot. I brought something I want everyone to try."

Granny made a grumbling sound as she hung her head in her hands. When Brian was in the kitchen, she said, "I was hoping he'd forget about that thing he brought."

"What is it?" I asked as I took a small—a very small—sip of my wine.

"Heaven only knows," she replied. "Something brown and hard. Smells awful, too."

Brian came out with a platter in his hands, an oval lump resting on the middle of it. He had a look of pride on his face as he set it down in the middle of the table. "I made it myself," he announced, slurring his words.

"I was afraid you'd trip," Granny said, letting me know she'd just expressed what she was hoping.

"What is it?" Mariella asked.

"Vegetarian meatloaf," he said.

"Vegetarian meatloaf? That's an oxymoron if I ever heard one," Mariella said with a chuckle.

"Oxy what?" Brian said, jumping back up from the table. "Are you calling me a moron?"

My dad stood up now, ready to do battle with my so-called date. "Calm down, boy," he said, then explained what an oxymoron was to Brian.

Brian just shook his head and said, "Oh. Why didn't you tell me what you meant rather than spout off those million dollar words?"

My sister, grandmother, and aunt each offered me a look of sympathy. It was painfully obvious I'd made a gross error in judgment by bringing Brian to my family's Thanksgiving dinner. But it was too late to do anything about it now, so I decided just to gut it out and try to make the most of it.

Being the polite sort of family we were each of us took a small slice of that vegetarian meatloaf Brian had brought. But one bite for each of us was more then enough. It tasted so bad that I had to drown it in the rest of my wine. Brian was too drunk to notice.

"So, Mariella, tell me about the art show you had last weekend. I hear it was a rousing success." I hoped this would take the attention off Brian and redirect the conversation.

But no—he wouldn't let that happen. "Art show?" Brian said with a sarcastic laugh. "Don't tell me you're one of those."

"One of what?" Mariella asked defensively.

"A hoity-toity artist, who sees things that aren't even there," Brian said in spite of the fact that I was now kicking him under the table.

"Ouch!" he cried. "Stop that. Can't you see I'm talking?"

I sucked in a breath and shook my head. Granny saved the moment by saying, "Mariella's hobby is art, and she does wonderful work. Tell us what you do for fun, Brian."

He belched and said he lived for sports. "Nothing like a good game of old-fashioned football," he said.

"You play football?" my dad asked, a hopeful gleam in his eye. My dad had played football back in his high school and college days.

"No way. I watch games on television. You wouldn't catch me down on a dirty field with a bunch of meatheads."

Granny abruptly changed the subject again. "Tell us about your job, Brian."

"Why?" he asked. "Wanna make sure I'm good enough for your granddaughter?"

I glanced at my grandmother to see her reaction, which was unreadable. I knew this meant a long lecture later.

Oh, well. I asked for it by bringing Brian here in the first place. Man, I wish I'd never listened to Lorna.

When it was time for dessert, Granny announced we had four different pies as well as a chocolate cake. Brian said he wanted a sliver of each. I couldn't even look at him; he'd made me so angry.

By now, most of us were drinking coffee, which seemed to be the perfect beverage to go with dessert. But not Brian. He shook his head, chugged more wine, and said, "I don't do coffee. Too much caffeine makes me jittery."

The way he slurred his words let me know that I needed to find a way to get the wine bottle away from him. But when I reached for it, he slapped my hand. I pulled back, stunned. This whole thing was getting totally weird, and I had no idea what to do next.

"More chocolate cake," he said, thrusting his dessert plate toward Granny.

"You like my chocolate cake?" she asked with the first sincere smile I'd seen on her face all day.

"Not really," he replied, belching again. "It's one of the few things I can digest at this table. You people don't know how to eat around here."

"I'll get it, Granny," I said as I hopped up from the table and grabbed his plate. "You come with me." I reached down with my free hand and grabbed Brian by the arm, nearly dragging him all the way to the kitchen with me.

"What's up with you?" he asked as he swayed and finally found himself leaning against the wall.

"I'm calling you a cab," I told him.

"A cab?" he asked as he tried to stagger toward me.

I moved, and he stumbled. Somehow, I managed to push him away from me in the nick of time—before he fell on top of me. That was all I needed—a drunken jerk on top of me in my grandmother's kitchen.

"Yeah, you're drunk and obnoxious," I said. "And I'm totally embarrassed by you."

"I embarrassed you?" he said. "I was just speaking my mind. Want me to go straighten it out?"

"No!" I said quickly. "Don't do anything."

He shrugged and slid down the wall to the floor. "Okay, if you really feel that way. I was just starting to like you and your family."

"You certainly have a strange way of showing it," I said. "Why do you say such obnoxious things?"

"I don't know," he replied. "I guess I'm not the kind of guy girls like."

"Not this girl," I said as I winced. I hated being cruel, but Brian had asked for it. Still, though, it went against my nature.

Brian didn't say anything, so I went over to the phone on the wall and lifted the receiver. I placed a call to the local cab company and told them the passenger would be waiting out front.

"I'll walk you out there," I told him.

"I don't wanna leave you here alone," he said. "I might not be the kind of guy you wanna date, but I did bring you here."

"That's okay," I told him. "I've been here alone before, and I can get back to my apartment by myself." Not only was Brian a drunk, jerky dork, but he was obviously not very bright.

Brian went back to the dining room while I grabbed the dish he'd brought.

He was still making obnoxious comments when I went to the door and gestured for him to come with me. "Let's go, Brian," I said. "We don't want to keep the cab driver waiting."

"Bye, Brian," everyone said at once. As I rounded the corner, right behind Brian, I thought I even heard Granny add, "Good riddance, Brian." I had to bite my lip to keep from smiling.

The cab was there in a couple of minutes. I opened the door, told him to take Brian home, then turned to leave. Brian reached out and grabbed my arm, pulling me toward him. He was puckered up like he wanted to kiss me. In one quick motion, I pulled free, thank goodness. A kiss from Brian would have put me over the edge.

"Bye, Brian," I said as I slammed the door. "And good riddance, indeed."

Before going back inside, I squared my shoulders and took a deep breath. I knew my family would be unmerciful with their teasing, so I needed to brace myself. And I was right.

"So, do I hear wedding bells?" Mariella said with a smirk.

"Brian and Faith, sittin' in a tree. . . ." my younger teenage brother started quipping.

"Y'all, be quiet," I said. "It would serve you right if I married Brian."

"Let's hope you never get that desperate," Granny said.

Placing my hand on my hip, I turned to her and said, "But I thought you were trying to marry me off."

"Not to someone like that," she said. "I'd rather see you stay an old maid." She quickly cast a glance over her shoulder at Mariella. "No offense, Mariella. I'm just trying to make my point."

"Your point?" I asked. "Which is?"

Granny put down the platter she'd picked up, placed both hands on her hips, and glared at me. "Don't think that you ever have to settle for just any guy, Faith. You're a smart, beautiful woman with a bright future. Men like Brian don't deserve a woman like you."

"The only reason I brought Brian to dinner was to get you to stop harping on me about not having a man in my life," I said.

"You did that for me?" Granny asked.

Suddenly, everyone at the table started laughing. Mariella was the one who spoke first. "Granny, maybe you should reconsider about Brian. He's not that bad."

Granny rolled her eyes and motioned me to follow her into the kitchen. I was right behind her.

As soon as we were alone, she gently placed one hand on my shoulder and said, "Faith, honey, don't ever do anything like that again. You scared me half to death."

"Scared you? Brian wasn't that bad."

Granny chuckled. "Oh, he was pretty bad. Kind of like every grandmother's worst nightmare."

"Well, sorry about that. I didn't mean to shake you up that much. I just thought you wanted me to meet Mr. Right and ride off into the sunset."

Granny shook her head. "Never mind about finding Mr. Right.

It's obvious that you don't even know where to start."

"Thanks, Granny," I said. "Now that I'm off the hook, let's go out there and enjoy the rest of the holiday."

"Oh, you're not off the hook," she said with a sly gleam in her eye. "Judy down the street has a nice grandson—"

"Granny," I said, casting her a warning look. Then I burst out laughing. Some things never change. One of them is my grandmother, who loves me and wants what's best for me.

A blind date for Thanksgiving. What was I thinking? I'll have to get Lorna back for this one, I thought as I made my way back to my family, knowing I'd be hearing about this one for a long, long time.

THE END

A CHANGE OF PLANS
The Hope Of A New Beginning Comes With An Unexpected Thanksgiving Guest.

I pulled the baking dish from the oven and set it on the stove. Two pumpkin halves lay catty-corner in the dish, releasing fragrant steam that felt good against my face. I peeled back the crisp rind with a fork and started spooning soft golden flesh into the food processor.

I sighed. One pumpkin—that's all I had to show from this year's neglected garden. When the kids lived at home, the house burst with pumpkins every fall. Even after carving jack o' lanterns and canning puree for muffins and pies, I always had pumpkins to give away to neighbors and friends. Back then, I was the envy of my social circle— the perfect homemaker with the perfect husband and family.

While the metal blade turned the cooked pumpkin to smooth mush, I looked around at the bright, spacious, family-friendly house where I'd spent sixteen happy years, cooking, sewing, entertaining, and raising kids. I still love it. But I'd count myself lucky if I could walk away the day after tomorrow and never lay eyes on it again.

I poured pumpkin puree into a bowl and spooned more chunks into the food processor. Tomorrow was Thanksgiving Day. My son Pierce, who lived a few hours away in Waco, would drive over in the morning with his wife and kids. Jackie, a college senior, and Austin, a freshman, were flying home together from up north. We'd settle in for a cozy day of food, football, and companionship. Thanksgiving was our family's favorite holiday, and I was determined to make this year's as wonderful as the years before.

I refused to listen to the nagging little voice that said this might be harder than I was willing to admit.

Last November, I'll never forget that day. I'd hardly finished stowing the turkey leftovers in the fridge when, after twenty-five years of what I thought of as a happy marriage, Don had announced that he was leaving me for a woman younger than our son.

I was blindsided. Over the years I'd seen this happen to friends and acquaintances; sometimes I was surprised, sometimes not. But I never, ever thought it could happen to me.

The next six weeks were an ugly blur of papers and signatures, lawyers and meetings, moving vans and tears. I swung hourly between anger, denial, and depression. Just after New Year's, the divorce became final. I felt chewed up and spat out. Don's betrayal didn't just wreck my future; it colored my past, casting doubt on twenty-five years of happy memories. It was like someone had taken all our family photo albums and dunked them in sewer water.

"You have to find a job, Mom," AnnaLynne said. "Child support won't last forever."

I knew she was right, but the thought of applications and interviews filled me with dread. I'd never held a serious job in my life—just part-time and summer stuff. Naively, I quit college at twenty to get married. Finishing my undergrad degree after nearly three decades off would be a huge undertaking; anyway, I needed money now.

My first day of job-hunting left me shaken. I didn't even speak the language of today's job market. My computer experience amounted to asking the kids to help me make labels for homemade jam, listening glassy-eyed as they attempted to teach me how to do it myself, and forgetting everything they said once the labels started screeching their way through the printer.

In desperation, I went to Josie, my old roommate at the University of Texas. Although our lives had taken different paths since college—I'd become a stay-at-home mom; Josie had opened a successful business—we stayed in touch. I didn't want to ask for favors, but I was starting to panic.

Dressed in my interview clothes and the first pair of heels I'd owned since 1984, I wore slicked-back hair and a full complement of makeup as I sat in Josie Laurent's office and told her about my fruitless job search. "I know my resume is skimpy, and I know I don't have the skills to be competitive in today's market—especially now, with unemployment at ten percent. But I really need a job. I'm willing to work hard, and I'll do whatever it takes to learn."

When I'd finished, Josie said, "Eve, we've been friends for thirty years. I'd love to help—I wish I could help—but right now, in this economy, I'm struggling to keep my business afloat without laying anyone off. I can offer you a part-time entry-level position for seven dollars an hour. That's the best I can do. Frankly, I think you'd do better going into business for yourself."

My heart sank, but I put on a brave smile. "I'm not an entrepreneur like you, Josie. I wouldn't know the first thing about starting a business. But really, thanks for your time."

"Wait, Eve. Hear me out. Have you ever thought about cleaning houses?"

"Well. . .no. I need to make serious money."

"How does twenty-five dollars an hour strike you? That's what I pay my housekeeper."

I stared at her. "Are you kidding?"

Josie smiled and shrugged. "It's worth the money to me. I can spend my time more profitably here, running my business. And plenty of people in neighborhoods like mine feel the same way."

She leaned forward. "You don't realize this, Eve, but you have a set of skills that certain people find very valuable. If you can find those people and learn to present yourself properly, you can earn a good living without having to get expensive training in something unfamiliar to you."

She pulled out a calculator and started figuring. "Housekeeping is a good business—flexible hours, little overhead. Once you establish a solid reputation among your clientele, you could expand—hire some college girls or young mothers to work under you. You could even branch out and do catering, special events."

I hardly heard her. I was still trying to wrap my mind around twenty-five dollars an hour.

Leaving Josie's office, I felt more optimistic than I had for months. AnnaLynne helped me make pretty flyers and business cards on the computer. I distributed these in upscale neighborhoods, put the word out to everyone I knew, and started taking calls.

Soon I had all the work I could handle. After twenty-seven years of managing my own busy household, I now spent my days maintaining order and cleanliness for other people.

But my worries weren't over. Besides my portion of the mortgage, I still had attorney's fees and a car payment. A massive chunk of Don's child support went to college tuition. After May, when AnnaLynne graduated, Don's monthly child support checks would stop. Before the divorce, I'd never thought about our money and how it fit into the big picture. I followed a budget for things like groceries and clothing and let Don handle the rest. Turned out, our finances weren't as robust as I'd thought. My share of our joint assets didn't amount to much. Retirement, which had once seemed many millennia away, loomed dark and ominous in the not-so-distant future.

Now, for the first time, I considered selling the house.

For sixteen years, I'd been saying and believing that this would be the last home I'd ever own. I'd envisioned it as a family homestead, the future setting for decades of Rockwellian holidays, with plenty of room for our kids and grandkids.

But that was a fantasy from another lifetime. Truth was, I had twelve years left on a mortgage whose payments I could barely cover. All the repairs and improvements Don and I had put off during the busy kid-raising years were growing urgent, and I didn't have time or money to deal with them. Don had been pressuring me to sell for months; he wanted his equity. And though it broke my heart to think of leaving, I knew I'd be better off in a small, low-maintenance place that would permit me to get along on my income and lay something aside for retirement.

A real estate agent came over and walked around criticizing. "The siding needs to be painted, and there's a cracked window pane in the garage. Oh, the colors in this kitchen are too dark! It's like a cave in here. And this countertop is worn out. You should replace it with something light. Granite would be best. Hmm—grime on the walls and scuffs along the baseboards. This bedroom wallpaper is soooo dated! And the edges are peeling. Strip it off and give the whole interior a fresh paint job. Look at these grubby paths in the carpet! It'll have to be replaced. Of course, you'll take down all these family photos. You want potential buyers to be able to imagine themselves living in the house, and they can't do that if you and your kids are grinning down at them from the walls. And it sure wouldn't hurt to update these light fixtures."

I listened, stunned, feeling like she'd said my haircut was dowdy and my outfit made me look fat. Suddenly my beautiful home seemed shabby and pitiful.

I couldn't afford to pay for these improvements myself, and Don refused to discuss it. "Just sell as-is and get what you can. I don't want to sink any more money into that place."

"But the agent says—"

"I don't care what the agent says. I'm not paying for new paint and countertops for a house I don't live in anymore."

The house went on the market in February. We had some showings, but no offers.

Then the bottom fell out of the housing market in our area. Almost overnight, our home's resale value plummeted. We'd be lucky to get back what we owed, much less make a profit.

Having worked through the emotional rigors of deciding to sell the house, I suddenly found myself stuck with it.

Don was furious. "If you hadn't shilly-shallied over putting the house on the market, we'd have sold it by now and made a profit!"

"I can't believe you have the nerve to whine to me, Don! You got off scot-free. You're in your little apartment without even a lawn to mow, while I'm stuck in a house that's falling down around me."

I had plenty to deal with besides the house. AnnaLynne had won a partial scholarship for basketball at the same university Jackie attended, and she had to arrive early for off-season conditioning. So in June, we loaded her stuff into my Suburban and drove north. I stayed the weekend at Jackie's apartment, and took the girls shopping and out to eat. I knew I couldn't afford to, but I so wanted to treat my daughters to a good time. While we laughed and talked, my mind ran a ticker tape on the cost of this trip, including spending money for the girls and their books, personal items, and meals since they were paying their own room and board and had student loans to cover what financial aid and scholarships did not.

The night after I returned, I dreamed I was alone in a dark ocean, exhausted from treading water, and about to go under. I woke up hyperventilating and covered with sweat. Foreclosure, bankruptcy, and poverty were like dark presences lurking in the shadows of my bedroom.

What if Don gets fed up and stops paying his share of the mortgage? What if I get sick and can't work? I'm not on Don's insurance anymore, and if I don't work, I don't get paid. One bad month could wipe me out.

I couldn't go back to sleep. I got up, walked around the empty house, and finally settled in Jackie's old room to work on the wallpaper. It was a pink and white floral pattern, with a border of ballet shoes. A week ago I'd gone over all the papered walls with a rented heat gun, which was supposed to melt the glue and make the wallpaper come off easily in big sheets. It hadn't worked. I had to pull the paper off in confetti-like shreds. I lay on my side on Jackie's bed, picking at the colorful wallpaper that had looked so bright and cheerful to me sixteen years ago. My shabby house was getting shabbier every day.

Suddenly the paper tatters ran together in a blur of salty tears. At this rate, it would take me years to get the house into shape. If only the church would organize a work day at my house and get some of these chores knocked out.-- My church friends knew about the divorce, of course; they'd made the usual sympathetic remarks and told me to let them know if there was anything they could do. But some barrier of pride or reserve kept me from taking this blanket invitation seriously. I was too embarrassed to ask for help, but I wouldn't have been ashamed to take it, if it had been given outright.

I felt like praying, but couldn't put the words together. All I could say was, "Oh Lord, help." So I said it, over and over.

The next day my head ached and my eyelids felt gritty and hot. I wanted to pull the covers over my head and stay in bed, but I couldn't afford to lose the work. All day, while I scrubbed, straightened, and swept, I envied my clients and their slate tile floors, granite countertops, huge incomes, and 401k's.

I dragged myself home, dropped my purse and keys on the counter, and popped a frozen dinner into the microwave. While it heated, I checked my email, hoping for a message or funny story to cheer me up. I got nothing but a Botox advertisement and a message from the church prayer chain.

URGENT! read the subject line. Young mother needs help.

"Well, so do I!" I shouted to the screen. "I don't have the

98

emotional energy to pray for someone else's crisis! I have enough problems of my own!"

But I forgot all that once I started reading the message.

It was about Marita, a single mother with a toddler. She'd attended the church for about a year. She was polite, but quiet. According to the email, the city had condemned her tiny duplex. She had two weeks to get out, with nowhere to go.

It wasn't hard to read between the lines. The address of the rented duplex belonged to a seedy part of town. Any mother willing to stay there must be unable to afford a decent place.

Suddenly my problems didn't seem so serious. I was worried about the mortgage and retirement; Marita was struggling to keep food on her table. I was fretting about home repairs; in two weeks, Marita wouldn't have any house at all.

Then it hit me. Why shouldn't she stay here? I've got plenty of space—too much. Marita and her baby can have Pierce's old room. It's safe and comfortable, and the house certainly isn't about to sell anytime soon.

I hesitated. Marita seemed steady and clean living, but I hardly knew her. Did I dare ask her into my home? Wasn't that taking too much on myself?

But wasn't I just wishing that someone else would step up and help me without waiting to be asked? Why shouldn't I do the same thing for someone who's worse off than I am?

I found Marita's number in the church directory and started dialing before I could change my mind.

Marita and her little boy, Joey, moved into Pierce's room. It was bigger than the room they'd shared in the duplex, it had its own bathroom, and Marita considered it the height of luxury. She paid me a small amount of rent, enough to maintain her self-respect and make a difference in my budget.

"You have such a beautiful home," she kept saying. "Thank you for sharing it with us."

We got along comfortably. Marita was cheerful and courteous, and more than willing to do her share of housework. The loss of privacy had worried me at first, but it turned out to be a non-issue. Marita worked at the hospital from noon to eight, so I seldom saw her or Joey except when our days off overlapped.

In spite of hard work and frugal living, Marita had almost no savings. Childcare costs ate up so much of her income. Privately, I wondered if she would ever get ahead. Poverty was such a trap.

Well, at least she and Joey have a decent roof over their heads and good food to eat. Lots of people are worse off.

One day, Marita made a proposition.

"My friend Suzy works at the hospital, too, from eight p.m. to four a.m. She has four-year-old twins, and she pays even more for childcare than I do. I was wondering, would you be interested in renting out your two other rooms to her? Suzy's a good person; she doesn't drink or do drugs or anything, and she pays her bills on time. I haven't brought it up with her yet, but I was thinking that if she and I lived together, we could trade off on childcare, and you would have some extra income, too."

I wasn't sure. Renting a room to someone I knew from church was one thing; taking in a stranger was something else.

I went to the hospital and met Suzy. She was a brisk, plainspoken woman with a good sense of humor. I liked her right away, and her supervisor gave her a glowing report.

She moved in at the end of the month.

Macy and Molly, the four-year-old twins, regarded my house with wide-eyed wonder. The many bedrooms, the spacious living areas, and the big yard filled with trees made it seem like a palace.

Fortunately all three children enjoyed peeling wallpaper.

Night after night, morning after morning, Marita and Suzy came home from the hospital, snatched a few hours of sleep, and took turns at housework and childcare. In spite of the grinding hard work and meager pay, I never heard them complain. They'd both seen harder times; they were grateful for steady work, a decent place to stay, and a chance to save money.

Don was horrified. "What do you think you're doing, Eve? Running a homeless shelter? Those welfare queens and their brats are going to wreck my house!"

"They aren't welfare queens, Don. They're hardworking, frugal women. They thank me every day for the opportunity to live here. And their children walk around the house like it's the Taj Mahal."

"Yeah, well, you just wait. They'll get used to it soon enough, and then they'll want more. Now that they know you're a soft touch, they'll hang around you forever, waiting for more handouts."

"They're not getting handouts now! They pay rent, and they keep the upstairs and the bathrooms sparkling clean."

"Just wait," Don repeated smugly.

I was furious. Don acted as if it wasn't even possible for someone with a low income to have a strong work ethic or a good character. I went a few more rounds with him, then hung up and went outside to take out my anger on the weeds.

In an irrational burst of springtime optimism, I'd put in a garden, blithely telling myself I could do the weeding and watering on weekends. It hadn't happened. I walked down the neglected rows, ashamed of the cracks in the ground and the weeds choking the tomato and pepper plants. At last I found a lone survivor: a pumpkin vine, struggling along valiantly with a single fruit.

I gave up the tomatoes and peppers for dead and watered the pumpkin. Every Thanksgiving since my marriage, I'd made pumpkin pies from fresh pumpkins. I was determined to do it this year, too.

Once the soil was soft, I went after the weeds. I was sitting on the ground, tugging at a stubborn taproot, the sun beating down on my neck, sweat running in my eyes, and my hair straggling into my face, when a deep voice said, "Excuse me, ma'am. Are you Mrs. Wintar?"

I looked up to see a pair of steel-toed work boots and jeans. I looked farther up, past a long, lean body to a tanned face with a scrubby beard and dark, solemn eyes. The man held a grimy baseball cap in his tough hands.

The weed came up all at once, spraying me with mud and sending me back on my haunches. I wiped my face with a dirty hand. "Yes, I'm Eve Wintar."

"Mrs. Wintar, my name's Owen Salinger. I've been doing some work for your neighbor down the road, Russ Astoria. . .been helping him with his fences and new barn and such. I'm looking for a place to stay, and Mr. Astoria mentioned that you're running a sort of boarding house."

Boarding house! Is that what the neighbors think?

"I wouldn't put it that way," I said stiffly. "I do have some friends staying with me right now, and they do contribute to the upkeep of the house. But the rooms are full. I'm sorry, but I don't have space for anyone else." But I wasn't sorry at all. It was one thing to rent rooms to Marita and Suzy; it would be something else altogether to take in a man off the street.

"Yes ma'am, I understand that. It's actually your garage apartment I'm interested in."

I stared blankly at him. I'd forgotten we even had a garage apartment—or, at least, the rudiments of one. But evidently Russ Astoria had remembered.

"It's really not an apartment," I said. "It's just an unfinished attic with plywood subflooring. It's wired and stubbed for plumbing, but that's all—no drywall, no kitchen, no running water. It's really not habitable."

His eyes crinkled in what might have been a smile. "Sounds like it would suit me fine. See, what I'd like to do is fix the place up in exchange for rent. I could do the work on evenings and weekends, when I'm not busy with my regular job. I'd pay for materials and do all the labor. All you'd have to do is pick out colors and fixtures. I'm a good carpenter. You can ask Mr. Astoria. He'll vouch for my character, too."

My head was spinning, and I didn't know what to say. "I'm going to have to think this over."

"Yes, ma'am. Take your time. If you want to reach me, just call Mr. Astoria."

With that, he put on his hat and walked back to the road. I brushed my hands off and went inside to call Russ.

"Owen is really solid," he said. "He's worked with me for eight weeks. Before that, he worked for my friend Steve, doing some trim carpentry. He does beautiful work, and I can't hardly get him to quit at night. I know he looks rough, but he's never given me any reason to think he drinks or does drugs or has any bad habits. Heck, he doesn't have time for bad habits. He gets up at dawn and works until bedtime. He's been living in Steve's mobile trailer, but Steve wants to use it this month, so Owen has to find someplace else."

In the end, even with Russ' glowing recommendation, I might not have taken a chance on Owen if Don hadn't made me so mad that day with his talk about welfare and handouts. Gleefully, I imagined giving him the news. Don, I've taken in a homeless man as a boarder. He looks like a recovering alcoholic, but he has a nice face, so I'm letting him stay here rent-free in exchange for some handyman work.

The unfinished garage attic was about a hundred and thirty degrees the day I showed it to Owen. I hadn't been inside it since the house was built. There was exposed insulation on the walls, and the plywood subflooring wasn't even nailed down.

"It's pretty rough," I said.

"I've lived in worse," Owen replied.

I bet you have, I thought. I wondered what his story was. Why did he work so hard and allow himself so few comforts? What was he running from?

The arrangement was a good deal for me. I didn't receive rent, but I was getting the garage apartment finished at no expense, and that might just help with resale. It surely couldn't hurt.

Owen spent a few days nailing down plywood, putting in plumbing fixtures, and installing a window unit. Then he moved in, and I more or less forgot him. I picked out a couple of paint colors from some chips he brought me, then washed my hands of the matter and told him to use his own judgment. I had too much on my plate to micromanage this project.

Now, several months later, I had no idea what progress he'd made, if any.

I set the container of pumpkin puree in the fridge, next to the plastic-wrapped lump of homemade pie pastry.

Suzy came downstairs in her uniform, ready for her shift. "The

102

twins are upstairs watching a video, and Joey's in his playpen. They should be fine until Marita gets here."

"All right. What's your plan for tomorrow?"

"Oh, I'll catch a few hours of sleep after I get off work, and then drive to my brother's. He's expecting us around noon. Marita's planning on leaving for her grandmother's at nine, I think."

We said goodbye, and Suzy left for work. As much as I liked Suzy, Marita, and the children, I was glad they had someplace else to be tomorrow. I'd have been hard pressed to come up with sleeping arrangements otherwise. I'd decided to put Pierce and Amy in Pierce's old room, the grandbabies in port-a-cribs in Jackie's old room, and AnnaLynne and Jackie in AnnaLynne's old room.

Now I was ready to focus on cleaning. Once I started, I couldn't stop. I pulled out seat cushions, vacuumed upholstery, and moved heavy furniture to get dust bunnies. When Marita came home, she commented on the scent of furniture polish in the air.

I didn't realize things had gotten so dirty! I should have started a week ago. I've been so busy cleaning other people's houses that I've neglected my own.

Once the living and dining rooms were finished, I returned to the kitchen and tackled the stovetop and the range hood, then pulled everything off the counters and wiped them down. It was two a.m. before I finally collapsed into bed, but the house was sparkling.

I was just drifting off when a thought jerked me wide-awake. Cranberries! I forgot to buy cranberries!

I felt so disappointed I almost cried. How could I have forgotten? I wanted so much for everything to be perfect tomorrow!

I considered getting up. Wal-Mart might still be open. But no, it would be foolish to sacrifice my few remaining hours of rest. Too exhausted to think about it anymore, I fell asleep.

I woke at four-fifteen when Suzy came home, and decided to get up. I was too excited to sleep anymore, and I'd set the alarm for five anyway.

I rolled out piecrusts while coffee brewed. I wanted to have the pies baked by seven-thirty so the oven would be free for the turkey. I worked fast, enjoying the cozy feeling of anticipation. I had everyone's favorite dishes—green bean casserole for Pierce, pumpkin pie for Jackie, extra dressing for AnnaLynne. In a few hours I'd call Pierce and ask him to pick up the cranberries on his way. Lots of grocery stores would probably be open a few hours this morning.

After dinner, we'd watch the game between the University of Texas and Texas A&M. The rivalry was an intense one, going back to 1894. Don and I had met at UT, and we'd watched the game every year since our wedding. Even when the kids were too little to understand, they'd joined in the yelling and cheering.

This will be a perfect day—a day that will make up for all the loneliness and stress of the past year.

I was just setting the pies on the cooling rack when the phone rang. It was Pierce.

"Hello honey! I'm so glad you called. I need you to stop by the grocery store on your way and pick up some cranberries."

Pierce sighed. "Actually, Mom, I'm afraid we're not going to make it at all today. The kids are sick with some vomiting and fever thing. Amy and I were up all night with them, and now Amy doesn't feel so great herself. I'm really sorry, Mom, but there's no way we can travel."

I did my best not to sound as disappointed as I felt. "Oh, honey, I'm sorry too. We'll miss you, but you're right to stay home. Kiss the babies for me, and tell Amy I hope she gets better soon."

The house seemed very quiet after we hung up. I stared at the phone, fighting tears. I'd counted on Pierce to carve the turkey, and I'd so looked forward to seeing him and Amy and the babies.

Well, no point dwelling on what can't be helped. At least I'll have the girls.

I went on cooking, determined to be cheerful. I'd just set the timer for the hard-boiled eggs when the phone rang again.

"Mom? It's Jackie. Have you been listening to the weather?"

"The weather?" I asked blankly. "No, why?"

"Well, we've been hit by an ice storm. We've had freezing rain all night, and it's supposed to get worse as the day goes on. Lots of power lines are down. We lost electricity around two o'clock this morning and haven't had it since."

"Oh, sweetie! Are you freezing?"

"We're warm enough. We've got wood for the fireplace, and so do most of the neighbors. The thing is. . .the airport has canceled all today's flights. We're stuck here until the weather clears."

At first I was too shocked to speak. Finally I said, "What will you do?"

"We'll manage. We're all in the same boat here, so some of us are pooling resources. I've got a dozen frozen pizzas, and the guys next door have chips, ice cream, and a charcoal grill. We'll grill the pizzas and hang out. AnnaLynne's here, by the way. She spent the night. She was all packed for our trip south, so she'll just weather the storm with me."

Tears stung my eyes. "You're eating grilled pizza for Thanksgiving dinner?"

"Well, it's better than eating it raw. We're better off than lots of

104

people, at least we have something to cook with. I'm just sorry to miss Thanksgiving at home. You'll have to record the UT game for us, okay Mom? Get Pierce to do it; he knows how."

I choked up. "All right," I managed to say. There was no point telling her Pierce wasn't coming, either. She was already more worried for me than for herself.

AnnaLynne got on the phone. "I'm really sorry, Mom. I wish we could be there. But don't worry about us, because we're fine. We've got plenty of food and plenty to do. Say hi to Pierce and Amy, and kiss the babies for us, okay? And we'll see you at Christmas break. That's only a few weeks away, you know."

"Yes, baby, I know. You and Jackie stay warm, and have a happy Thanksgiving."

Happy Thanksgiving. The words rang hollow in my ears after we hung up. I looked around the kitchen. Every counter overflowed with the usual disarray of a holiday meal in the making. The turkey and dressing were in the oven. Giblets simmered on the stove. The sweet potato and green bean casseroles were in the fridge, ready to pop in the oven after the turkey came out. A big three-wicked candle stood on the table, surrounded by the bittersweet wreath I'd made when the kids were small. The whole house waited in festive, sparkling-clean readiness.

I dropped onto a barstool and rested my head against the wall, suddenly exhausted.

But the meal still had to be cooked, even if I would be the only one here to eat it. I refused to think about how many weeks worth of leftovers would be crammed into my fridge by the end of the day.

When Marita and Suzy came downstairs, they found a smiling landlady and a fresh pot of coffee. I wouldn't, couldn't, tell them my problems and have them feel sorry for me. I barely had my emotions under control; sympathy would push me over the edge.

"The house looks beautiful!" Marita said. "Smells great, too."

"Thank you! Would you like some coffee? How about some muffins? They're pumpkin; I made them yesterday."

Suzy took a muffin. "Mmm! Eve, you are an amazing woman."

The kids were dressed and ready, their backpacks stuffed with toys and snacks. They munched muffins at the kitchen bar.

"Well, ladies, are you looking forward to seeing your families?" I asked brightly.

Marita nodded. "My grandmother practically raised me, and she hasn't seen Joey since he was born. She can't travel anymore, and until I came to live here, I couldn't ever save enough gas money to go to her. She's so excited that we're coming at last."

Suzy was going to see her brother. "He's really my half-brother, the son of my ex-stepfather. We were close when we were kids, but our childhood was such a mess. Our parents and step-parents had so many issues, that between one thing or another, we lost touch. I was so glad when he looked me up a few months ago."

My feelings were mixed. I was happy for Suzy and Marita, but I would have welcomed an excuse to invite one or both of them to stay home with me.

Then they both said, as they so often did, how grateful they were to be living at my house. We all wished each other a happy Thanksgiving, and they loaded up and drove off.

After the sound of their car engines had faded away, I dropped onto the sofa and wept. Then, worn out with work and disappointment, I fell asleep.

I woke all at once, feeling that something had startled me. The shadows in the room had shifted. I looked at the clock. It was after eleven.

I heard it again: a knock at the back door.

I ran my hands through my hair and answered the door. Owen stood outside, holding a beautiful cut-glass dish of something red.

"Mrs. Wintar, here's a little cranberry conserve to add to your table today. I surely am grateful to you for giving me a place to stay and work to do, and I hope you have a happy Thanksgiving."

I was so shocked I could hardly manage to thank him. He smiled and left without another word.

I set the dish on the table. The autumn sunshine made it glow like a jewel.

Cranberry conserve! Of all things! I wonder where it came from. Does he have a daughter visiting, or a sister, or maybe a lady friend?

Ever since I'd first met Owen, I'd assumed he was estranged from his family. He had such a sad, solitary look. I had the feeling that he had some issues, deep-seated issues. But all this was just an impression. I really knew next to nothing about him.

Well, it's time to change that.

I climbed the stairs to the garage apartment and knocked on the door. Owen answered, looking as surprised as I must have five minutes ago.

"Hi there," I said. "I suddenly realized I haven't seen the apartment since before you moved in. I thought I'd take a look. That is, if I'm not interrupting your Thanksgiving dinner."

He opened the door wide and waved me inside. "Oh, there's time yet. As you can see, I haven't started my repast."

I walked in and beheld a perfect little jewel of an apartment. Doors, windows, and baseboards were neatly trimmed; crown molding ran along the ceiling and ceramic tiles covered the floor. A worn plaid armchair stood in one corner, using a steamer trunk as a coffee table. The nice, convenient little kitchen had honey-oak cabinetry and granite countertops. Granite countertops!

Owen smiled sheepishly. "I know. I got carried away. Hope you don't mind."

"Mind? Are you kidding? You paid for the materials. Anyone can see I came out way ahead on this deal. It looks wonderful."

"Thank you. I enjoyed the project, and I'm just glad you gave me the opportunity. The work has been very. . .therapeutic."

Mm-hm, I thought. Issues.

There was something almost sad about the immaculate tidiness of the little apartment. The drop-leaf table was set for one, with a box of crackers, a small bowl of cranberry conserve, and what looked like a tub of crab dip from the supermarket deli.

"Are you alone today?" I asked.

"Yes, ma'am." No excuses, no explanations.

"In that case, how would you like to have Thanksgiving dinner with me?"

"Oh, that's awfully good of you, Mrs. Wintar, but I couldn't possibly impose."

"I'm afraid there's nothing to impose on. My family's not coming. My grandbabies are too sick to travel, and my daughters are iced in up north. It would be a kindness for you to join me and help me make a dent in the turkey."

Something softened around his eyes. "In that case, Mrs. Wintar, I'll come and gladly. What time will dinner be served?"

"Please, call me Eve. Give me an hour to shower and change, and then come on over. We'll watch some football, and eat around two. Tennessee and Detroit kick off at twelve-thirty."

Suddenly it felt like Thanksgiving again. I dressed up, brushed on some mascara, and put my hair in a flipped-up kind of style. I was just lighting the big candle on the table when I heard Owen's knock.

He looked so different, that for a moment, I thought it was someone who just looked like Owen. A brother, maybe—a younger, happier brother, with dark hair slicked back from a high forehead and a strong, clean-shaven chin with a dimple in it.

A brother wearing a maroon-and-white Texas A&M jersey.

He grinned and lifted his hand. A class ring glittered on his finger. "Class of eighty-five. School of Engineering."

We didn't watch much of the NFL game, but it made a cozy background noise while we chatted in the kitchen. Here I got another surprise: Owen used to own a business in Dallas—a pretty prosperous business, from the sound of things.

How did a successful businessman with an engineering degree

from A&M get reduced to living in a garage apartment and doing odd jobs?

At one-thirty the turkey came out of the oven, golden-brown and sizzling. I spooned out some pan juices for gravy, while Owen competently chopped hard-boiled eggs at the kitchen island.

When everything was ready, we both laughed to see the table laden with a nineteen-pound turkey and half a dozen huge casserole dishes, but only two places set.

There was an awkward moment just before we began. Don used to pray before the meal, and I'd meant to ask Pierce to do it this year.

Owen must have sensed my uncertainty, because he suddenly bowed his head and began. "Thank you, Lord, for the blessings of food and drink and material comforts, of meaningful work, of family and friends, and most of all, Your loving care. Amen."

He quietly took charge of the carving, too, and filled my plate with thin, juicy slices of white meat.

He complimented my cooking, and I complimented his. "This cranberry conserve is delicious. Did you make it yourself?"

"Yes. It's my wife's recipe."

I looked up, startled. Wife—not ex-wife.

After a moment, he went on, "I lost my family in an accident two years ago, my wife and four kids."

"Oh, Owen." I didn't know what to say. "I'm sorry."

"Yeah. It kind of unhinged me, losing them all at once. I hurt all the time. I used to take my clean laundry out of the dryer and dump it on Nora's side of the bed and leave it there, so I wouldn't feel like I was sleeping alone. Finally I sold the house and the business and just took off. I'd put myself through college doing carpentry work, so I went back to that. It was good for me, working with my hands. It helped get my head straight."

I felt terrible. Ever since I'd first laid eyes on Owen, I'd been making assumptions about him.

We talked a long time about his family, then he asked about mine. When he heard about Don, Owen shook his head. "He doesn't understand what he's throwing away. He will one day, when it's too late."

I told him about my trouble with the house. "It's been on the market nine months, and we haven't had one offer. I know it needs work, but Don refuses to put any more money into the place. Of course, the market's bad right now, but I'm sure it would help to have the house ready to move into."

Owen thought. "Maybe we could make an arrangement. The garage apartment's finished, and my other construction job is winding down. I've about reached the end of my money. I'm not really broke, but most of my assets are tied up in investments, so at the moment

I'm cash-poor. What if I did the work on your house in exchange for rent? It wouldn't cost you much out-of-pocket, so maybe you could swing it without Don contributing. And maybe by the time the house is in shape, the market will have recovered some."

What a perfect idea! I agreed at once. Owen walked around the house, noting everything that needed work, including really nitpicky things that even the real estate lady hadn't noticed. His eyes brightened, and he started talking faster. He seemed excited by the prospect of a big job.

Owen helped me with the dishes. I packed plenty of leftovers for him to take back to his place. We crammed my fridge and freezer full, then settled down in the living room to watch the Dallas game.

Pierce called at halftime. The babies were better, but Amy was miserably ill. "But you know what she said?" Pierce asked. "She said she was grateful to have such a warm house and comfortable bed to be sick in, and such a nice husband to take care of her. How's that for a wife?"

"She's a keeper," I said. "Don't you forget it."

"No," he said seriously. "I won't. Oh! The kids are calling me. I'd better run. Happy Thanksgiving, Mom. Say hi to the girls for me."

I smiled. He didn't know about his sisters' change in plans, much less about the man in my living room.

I called the girls. They were obviously having a blast eating their grilled pizza, roasting weenies before the fireplace, and playing board games with the guys next door.

"Did you tell Pierce to record the game?" Jackie asked.

"Pierce's not here. Amy and the babies are sick, so they had to stay home."

"Mom!" she wailed. "You're all alone?"

"No, I have a guest. One of the renters."

"Which one, Marita or Suzy?"

"Neither. It's Owen. I don't think you've met him."

"Mother!" she shrieked. "Are you renting a room to a man?"

Owen was staring at the television, but his lips twitched, so I knew he'd heard Jackie's outburst.

"Calm down, dear. Owen rents the garage apartment."

"Garage apartment? We don't even have a garage apartment."

"We do now. It's lovely."

Anna Lynne was yelling for a turn on the phone. When she got on, she didn't waste any time. "What's going on, Mom? Are you taking in male boarders? Who is this man?"

"His name is Owen. He's staying in the garage apartment and doing some work for me."

"Is he cute?"

My cheeks burned. "Well. . ."

"He is, I can tell by your voice. Will we meet him at Christmas?"

I studied Owen's strong profile. "I think you might."

Just before seven, I went to my room and came back wearing an orange-and-white UT jersey.

"All ready for kickoff!" I said.

We had a hilarious time during the game, cheering, jeering, catcalling, and singing inflammatory unofficial fight song lyrics at the top of our lungs.

It was late when Owen left with his bag of leftovers. "Thank you, Eve, for a wonderful holiday. This is the most fun I've had in a long time."

"Me too. Thanks for coming."

"How about we head over to Home Depot next week and put together a materials list for the work on the house?"

"Fine. I'm off all day Tuesday."

"Would ten o'clock be all right? And maybe I could take you to lunch afterwards."

I felt a pleasant little jolt of surprise. "I'd like that."

Suddenly Owen looked shy. "Well, good night, and thanks again."

It wasn't the holiday I'd planned, but I liked how it had turned out. I had so much to be thankful for: the kids, my work, Marita and Suzy, and a newfound spirit of hope for the future.

And of course, a new friend.

THE END

A THANKSGIVING
HOOK-UP IN THE CITY
Joined Two Lonely Holiday Hearts

Most people like Thanksgiving Day. It's a day to spend with family and loved ones. A day to entertain and feel like all is right with the world. I mean, what's not to like? The turkey and stuffing, honey glazed ham, and gazillion side dishes like macaroni and cheese, cranberry sauce, collard greens, corn on the cob, and mashed potatoes. It was an eater's heaven. I would go on a diet two weeks before the day—just to eat like I wanted to—especially my Aunt Bunny's bourbon pecan pie, and my sister Charlotte's sweet potato pie.

The tradition in my family after my parent passed away was for the four of us women to cook for the men—assorted cousins and nephews. It was a welcoming place to make sure that no one was left alone. My two married sisters always participated—even though it meant that their husbands had to join in with our crazy lot instead of spending the day with other family members.

After a long day of cooking, the sixteen of us would eat for hours. We cooked like we were feeding an army, because in a lot of ways, it felt like we were.

I'm the youngest of three daughters . . . and sadly the unmarried, childless one. Thanksgiving conversation usually started off about the basketball game, but ended with "So Chandra, I was wondering if you'd like to meet a buddy of mine." Despite my best efforts, I was looked upon like I was the hunchback of Chicago. Not because of any physical attribute, but because an unmarried woman in my family was sort of an abomination.

Basically, I was pitied because of my nonexistent love life. And worse, thought of as totally incapable of finding my own darn dates!

My droves of well-intentioned cousins and uncles saw my husbandless status, as a sin that was something right under "Thou Shalt Not Kill." Sometimes, I thought during our gatherings that I should have the letter A on my forehead, not for being an adulterer, that was not my style, but for alone.

So here we were again. Cooking, talking, and laughing, but I knew it was coming. Another year had gone by, and I hadn't made any sort of engagement notice. Another year had gone by, and I didn't even have a fiancé on the backburner waiting to burst forth to rescue me from a fate worse than death. I was twenty-six, and I hadn't popped out my first baby. Whoa! Would the world stop spinning on its axis?

Aunt Bunny, as everyone called her—real name Belinda—was pouring a liberal amount of vinegar in the greens when she said it. Yeah . . . it. "

So, Chandra . . .I was thinking . . . maybe you should sell your eggs to infertile couples. Since you're probably not going to use them. At least, you could make some money. Then, you could buy a car that has air conditioning."

My sister, Charlotte, nearly choked on the sip of soda she'd just taken.

"Aunt Bunny, please! Are you trying to kill me?"

Bunny looked at her with one raised eyebrow. It was the best impersonation of Dr. Spock I'd ever seen, but she was serious.

"Charlotte. I'm just trying to help. You young girls have no appreciation for the wisdom of your elders."

My oldest sister, Charlene, had long taken on the role of prankster. Unusual for the eldest child, but she took her role seriously. I nearly wet myself when she uttered for my ears only, " If only the wisdom was dispensed with a little less gin, it might be worth something!"

I slapped her arm—hard. The last thing in the world I wanted was to get Aunt Bunny started. She would fuss until the proverbial cows came home! I didn't have the patience or enough alcohol in my system to deal with it, today.

My week at work had been long and hard. We had a major project to finish before everyone took off for a couple days rest and relaxation. So today, for just once, just one Thanksgiving Day, I wanted to be left alone. I longed to have my family accept me for being just me: single and loving it. Yes, I wanted a husband and kids one day, but I planned to continue to build my career first.

My head was beginning to throb. I didn't want to appear grateful for their meddling. Didn't want to smile when I really wanted to ring Uncle Joe's neck. Why was it so impossible to believe that I was okay with being single, and was in no rush to have children? I missed the class that said we all had to behave and do the same things in life.

Now, instead of enjoying the time with my sisters and aunt, I was pissed. Charlotte, who knew me like the back of her hand, tried to help me out. She said, "Aunt Belinda, times have changed. Women work outside the home, run for political office, drive cars and don't have to wait hand and foot on some man. Lord knows even my Neanderthal, Gregory, cooks, and even washes dishes. Quit giving 'Little Bit' such a hard time. When the right man comes along, she'll know what to do. And if they want to make a long-term commitment, I'll be right there to make sure that she doesn't embarrass us with some butt-ugly wedding theme!"

I rolled my eyes at my sister. She was doing fine until she got to the last part. I shook my head to myself, I should have known better. As much as I loved her, she was in cahoots with the rest of the gang. She wanted me married with children so we could swap clothes and talk about our little darlings. I sighed to myself, maybe they were right. Maybe I was fighting against it too hard because the thought that I would actually like all this darned conformity was scary.

Truth be told, there was a young man that I hadn't worked up the nerve to say hello to at the office. He always looked great and smelled even better. Now, he was someone that I'd like to get to know better! Great body, perfectly evident in his designer suits, great smile—which he did often I noticed, and wonderful couture. He was the whole package. Neat hair, neat nails on long, well-proportioned hands, neat clothing, and neat briefcase. I watched him in our snack area one day . . . okay, so every chance I got.

As I conjured up a mental picture of him, I temporarily forgot about Aunt Bunny's comment. I was lost in my imaginings of him for a few seconds. His name is Alex Carmichael. Sometimes when I was really bored, I would doodle his name in the corners of my papers, pretty high school behavior and pretty pathetic, but my dream visions of him were enough to keep my hormones in high gear.

Unfortunately, it appeared that my aunt wasn't finished yet. Another comment about my marriage-less state by Bunny brought me back crashing back to the harsh reality of this Thanksgiving. There was no peace, and there wouldn't be any escape.

I toyed with the idea of using an escort service. I would buy some good-looking, probably gay guy, to be my cover story. He could be tall, dark and handsome, and totally unavailable!

With a heavy sigh, I placed the first of four large pans of macaroni and cheese in the oven, then I prepared to fix the second pan. I was determined not to give in to my aunt's alcohol influenced opinions.

Charlotte, or Charley, as we called her, handed me the cooked elbow noodles. I mixed cup one of six cups of cheese into them when the doorbell rang, again. The so-called men of the house were having a rousing good time in the family room, and of course, no one bothered to move toward the door. I sighed in frustration, put the cheese down and huffed my way to the door.

I couldn't imagine who it could be, though, because all the single cousins and my two brothers-in-law were already sitting in the family room of my aunt's house. The usual suspects were in place—so if this was some new freeloading friend of my lovable but useless cousins, I didn't know what I would do.

I snatched it open with a vengeance, daring this new "visitor" to be someone other than family.

The air whooshed out my chest. I couldn't believe my eyes. Why in the world was Alex Carmichael at my door? Okay, my aunt's door.

I had flour on my face, apron, and probably in my hair, too. I tried to fix myself up, but it was a pretty hopeless cause. I was a mess, but I was with family, and I was working hard!

The floor didn't open up and just swallow me up, which seemed like a miracle. I wanted to die of embarrassment. There was the object of all my desires . . . physical ones anyway, standing in front of me in all his fineness, and I was . . . well . . . not in my fineness at all. And feeling kinda low because of Aunt Bunny's tirade against me on top of that.

I looked down because I couldn't stand the thought of trying to make eye contact with him. The warmth of his laughter was almost too much for me to bear. It was so open, so inviting. I smothered the smile that wanted to turn up my lips. This was terrible, but I couldn't help thinking how funny this whole situation was at the moment. I mean, I'd been thinking about Alex for weeks, and now, here he was on one of the most special days of the year. At my aunt's house— no less.

"Umm . . . can I help you?"

My voice sounded high-pitched and nervous to my ears.

"What a nice surprise, Chandra. I didn't expect to see you, today."

He extended his hand as if we spoke all the time. And how did he know my name? He was just an office fantasy! "Happy Thanksgiving. Charlotte and Gregory Watkins invited me. I know Greg from the gym where we play racquetball twice a week. Don't tell me you know him, too?"

I stood listening to the deep bass of his voice. It wasn't until he stopped talking, but I didn't stop staring that it occurred to me to let the poor man in.

And with it being Thanksgiving in Chicago. I was letting all the cold air in and the heat out. I stuttered and stammered.

"Oh, come in, come in. I guess I'm a little surprised too. No one mentioned anyone else coming, so I didn't know what to expect when I opened the door. This is a pleasant surprise, though. Let me get your jacket." Hot damn, he smelled and looked great.

"Greg is my brother-in-law, and Charlotte is one of my older sisters."

I led him toward the family room where everyone was waiting. As soon as I entered the room ready to make the introduction, I saw Uncle Joe and Greg make eye contact. Okay now, I was pissed again. This was a set-up. But how did they know that I was even remotely interested in Alex?

Charlotte, Charlene, and Aunt Bunny came out of the kitchen just

114

then to see who had come to the door. As if they didn't already know. I was seething inside, but I couldn't let them know how upset the situation had made me. The vultures would feed off my discomfort for the rest of the evening. I made introductions again, while Charlotte came to hug Alex, then scooted back to the kitchen. Bunny tried to think of some reason for me to stay for a bit to chat, but because I was right in the middle of making more macaroni and cheese, she was temporarily thwarted.

In the kitchen, I wiped the sweat from my brow. Had the temperature really increased a hundred degrees or was it my hormones?

"Calm down girl. He's just the finest, sweetest thing since Godiva Chocolates, but it's cool."

"Oh wee! Now I see why Charlotte invited him. He is too fine."

"Charlene, do you guys think that you'll stop trying to set me up? I mean, this is bordering on harassment—or the very least, some form of mental persecution. Why did Charlotte have that poor man come over here, today? Isn't today supposed to be about family and tradition?"

Charlene had the good sense to be embarrassed. I watched as she shifted from foot to foot.

"Chandra, I know that you think that we are just a bunch of meddlesome relatives, but we love you. We just want you to be happy. I won't apologize for that. Since you and John broke up last year, you seem to have cut yourself off from the world. I can't just stand by while you dwindle away. What kind of sister would I be?"

I went back to my cooking, stirring the sweet potatoes for my pie with a vengeance. I had to grit my teeth for a few seconds before I could even talk again.

"But that's the thing. Yes, my break-up with John was hurtful. He left me for someone else. I had to learn to deal with it, but I haven't shut myself off, I'm just doing my own thing. I enjoy my time alone when I'm at home. No one is competing for my time, I can take a bubble bath, read a book, go shopping whenever I want to do those things. I don't have to synchronize my watch to meet with someone, or check with my man to see if he wants to go to the movies with me. I'm free to do what I want, and believe me, despite what you think, I'm not falling apart!"

Charlene sat down at the kitchen table with a slight smirk. She listened, but there was a certain look of disbelief on her face. I felt as if I needed to convince her that I really was okay, but despite anything that I might say, her mind wouldn't be changed. Aunt Bunny had me selling my eggs, Charlene didn't believe me, and Charlotte was inviting any eligible man that she could over to the house for me to meet. It was Thanksgiving, but all of a sudden I didn't feel like I had much to be thankful for. I looked around the kitchen, with a bitter taste in my mouth. We were in here cooking out butts off for those ungrateful men who would utter words of thanks between farts and burps. All of sudden I couldn't take it anymore. I very calmly finished putting the ingredients of my sweet potato pie into the crust, placed it in the oven, dusted myself off and headed toward the door.

As I walked through the family room, I noticed that Aunt Bunny was holding Alex hostage. I wondered if she knew that her wig was slightly askew?

He looked up at me, a slightly mischievous smile on his face, as I walked by. His eyes seemed to question where I was going, but since his lips didn't utter the words, I simply shut the door behind me. My raggedy sedan was in the driveway. Aunt Bunny's words echoed in my ears. Dammit, I could afford a car with air conditioning, but I was saving for a particular car. I would never tell her that I wanted a Lexus RX 330. She would view it as a waste of money for a vehicle that was too big for one person. She never gave me credit for knowing my own mind, so why should I tell her my hopes and dreams. I didn't want her or my sisters raining on my parade. I had enough to afford the L-E-X, but I was still working on the U and S. I went to the lot every month to scope out my midnight blue SUV with the leather interior, satellite radio, heated seats, and six-disc CD changer. In another year, I would buy my own home, so what was I doing so wrong?

I sat in the car for five minutes trying to get up the nerve to actually drive away. I could head back to my apartment, but for what? I'd have to take the phone off the hook because it would ring constantly.

I climbed into the driver's side, then I simply put my head on the wheel. I wasn't going anywhere. Who was I kidding? I'd be right there at the table listening to the tall tales, laughing and drinking with my family just like in years past. I felt like a wuss!

Tears filled my eyes but didn't fall. Maybe the melancholy was because at times like these, even though it was wonderful to be with everyone, it made me miss my parents. Maybe I just wanted to be around folks who would love me unconditionally. My last memory of them was of the five of us sitting around the dinner table. We had a great dinner, because Mom was such a great cook, then afterwards went to bed as usual.

By 3:00 a.m., I remember waking up to sirens, screams, and hands yanking me from my bed. I couldn't see anything, but a six-year-old knew what fire was, and days later, I knew what the two coffins signified. One or both of my parents who were heavy smokers had fallen asleep with a cigarette and set the bed on fire. A careless accident changed my life forever . . . all that was safe and good in my world came crashing down around me.

Aunt Bunny and Uncle Joe helped the three of us pick of the pieces of our lives, but our lives were never the same again. Love was always scary—something temporary or not to be trusted. Love was something—just like with John, which could go away any minute.

Twenty years later with a house full of family not twenty yards away, I was sitting in my unmoving car ready to cry.

A loud tap on the window nearly made me jump out of my skin. My eyes flew open in surprise, I guess as much from being startled as scared. I thought they would at least give me a few minutes to get myself together—but it wasn't my aunt or my sisters. When I opened my eyes, I was staring straight into the worried looking eyes of Alex Carmichael.

I reached for a tissue from the box that I had sitting in the passenger seat, and tried to fix my face. I was looking more of a mess now, than when I first answered the door to let him in—this was definitely not the kind of first impression that I wanted to make.

Alex tapped on the window again.

"Are you okay?"

I nodded, then I rolled down the window.

"I'll be fine. I just needed a minute to gather myself. I think I'm feeling a little bit overwhelmed right now."

Alex bent his knees so that he could talk to me at eye level. He didn't seem bothered at all that we were carrying on this conversation through the car in the cool temperatures of November in Chicago.

"So, let me guess. I wasn't invited over here today out of the goodness of Greg's heart? I'm sorry if I made you feel uncomfortable. Are you sitting out here because of me?"

Now, I was feeling really terrible. "Alex, it's cold out there. Come sit beside me."

He stood up to come around the car, giving me one more heady whiff of his cologne. I inhaled deeply as he came around. I unlocked the door for him, and pushed it open. He sat down quickly—accidentally brushing up against me. The heat from his touch immediately warmed me up.

"Alex, I'm so sorry for my family's antics. They shouldn't have duped you in order to feed you. We're not usually so brazen or so dishonest."

He waved his hands in a dismissive gesture.

"Think nothing of it. I was having a good time in there—Your family is . . . hmmm . . . quite colorful."

"That's a great way to put it. We're a bunch of loons, but

117

generally speaking, harmless. So what's your story Alex Carmichael? I've seen you at the office over the last few months. Did you just transfer to the Chi-Town area?"

He looked down, and then back up at me.

"Something like that. I moved here from Detroit almost a year ago. Most of my extended family is there, but I'm an only child, and I lost both parents two years ago. After the company offered me the chance to transfer, I jumped on it. I guess I wanted to start over again where the memories weren't so fresh. I'm starting to get out more now . . . starting to live a bit more. I accepted Greg's invitation because I thought it might be easier to deal with Thanksgiving Day away from my immediate family."

"Alex, I'm sorry to hear that. It's been several years since my sisters and I lost our folks, and the memories are becoming a blur, but I still miss them, everyday. I don't want to ruin this for you, so why don't we go back in. I'm game if you are."

Alex laughed.

"Your family is precious. I can see how much they care about you, but I'd like to stay here with you for a little bit if you don't mind."

"I don't mind at all. I could use some more shoring up before I go back in for more of Aunt Bunny's wisdom. Thanks for being so understanding."

"This is the longest conversation that we've ever had. I've watched you in the lobby, or sometimes as you come in or out from lunch, but I never had the nerve to introduce myself. Kind of lame, huh?"

I laughed. He wasn't the only one who was lame. We'd been watching each other from afar for months. This was ridiculous.

"I don't think that's lame. Dating is hard these days. I know I've kissed way too many frogs in my day. Sometimes, I just think that it's easier to remain alone. I'm happy that my sister has Gregory, and Charlene has Herbie, and Aunt Bunny has Uncle Joe, but I like my single life."

Alex blinked slowly.

"So does this mean that dinner is out of the question? Not today's dinner, but maybe just a quiet dinner for two? I'd like to get to know you better if you'll let me, Chandra."

"Dinner is definitely not out of the question, Mr. Carmichael. I would love to go out with you."

"Good, how about Sunday? We'll probably need from now until then to digest all the wonderful dishes that you and your family are cooking. You know, the one thing that I was struck by once I entered the room, was how much love I could sense in the house. Aunt Bunny seems to have made a very warm and comfortable environment, here. I suppose it can become overwhelming if you have to deal with it all the time; but frankly, I appreciate it."

He held my hand in his.

"So now that I have charmed you into seeing me again, how about we go back inside? I hear you make a mean macaroni and cheese."

His broad, brilliantly white smile made me forget why I'd even come outside. Maybe he was right. My family was precious to me, and despite all their interfering, they just wanted me to be happy—I decided then to stop being the turkey, and appreciate my family for their concern.

Alex and I walked back into the house hand-in-hand. I knew that I would be grilled as soon as I entered the kitchen, but I wasn't worried about it, anymore. I had a date with the object of my fantasies—Alex Carmichael. He kissed me lightly on the cheek before he let my hand go. I floated to the kitchen under the watchful eyes of Aunt Bunny with a big, wide smile on my face. "Thank you, Aunt Bunny."

And this time, I really meant it!

THE END